LITTLE VALLEY

Raymond Otis. *Photograph by Ernest Knee*

LITTLE VALLEY
Raymond Otis

Afterword by Marta Weigle

A Zia Book

UNIVERSITY OF NEW MEXICO PRESS
Albuquerque

Library of Congress Cataloging in Publication Data

Otis, Raymond.
    Little valley.

    (A Zia book)
    Reprint of the 1st ed. published in 1937 by Cresset Press, London.
    Bibliography: p. 282
    I. Title.
PZ3.0889Li 1980 [PS3565.T5]   813'.54   79–56813
ISBN 0–8261–0534–2

Afterword © 1980 by the University of New Mexico Press. All rights reserved. Manufactured in the United States of America. Library of Congress Catalog Card Number 79-56813. International Standard Book Number 0-8263-0534-2

This volume contains the complete text of the first edition, published in 1937 by the Cresset Press, Ltd., London, England.

PART ONE

CHAPTER I

OLD Pablo was dying.

Juliano's wife came down to the edge of the field and called to him. "*El abuelo esta mal,*" she said. "He asked for you. You'd better come."

And Juliano went up to the house in his bare feet, his legs plastered with mud to his knees. In those days a man really got into the earth when he irrigated his fields.

On reaching the house, Juliano went straight to the room where his father lay—they called him grandfather now, because so many grandchildren running about made it seem foolish to call him father. Into the darkened room Juliano went and a glance at the old man told him that Rosa was right—the end was not far off. Pablo lay back on his pillow and looked dead already, such was the pallor of his skin and the great hollows in his cheeks. But he was breathing faintly and as Juliano took the vacant chair beside his bed, the lips moved. "I want to speak to my oldest son."

Juliano stood up and with a nod dismissed the

dozen or more black-shawled women who had been sitting in a line of chairs along the walls, who now, like a procession of sombre ravens, marched out of the room. Juliano returned to the bedside and, placing his lips close to the old man's ear, said: "It's Juliano."

For reply, Pablo groped for his son's hand, found and held it, silently.

The mud on Juliano's legs was beginning to dry, pulling at the hairs as it contracted; and the son, while he waited for his father to speak, picked off chunks of mud with one hand, grimacing at the sharp little pains. Pablo, his eyes shut, was breathing slowly, unevenly. Juliano watched his lips—tired lips. Nothing in particular ailed the old man—he was just tired, worn out. He had lain down to die as a younger man lies down to sleep. He seemed to be in no pain, nor to regret overmuch his departure.

His lips were moving again—Juliano leaned closer to them.

"I have an old gun—you know? I bought it many years ago from a soldier at Fort Marcy. It is a good gun. Take it. It is for you, Juliano. Everything else you divide equally among you. My land, my house. But you should always farm the land together, you and your brothers. It is cruel—it will beat you if you don't. Farm it as one piece—never mind which owns it—and share equally in it. This much I have learned in my life. Do as I say, and the land will never harm you."

Juliano sat beside the bed for a long time after his father stopped speaking, for the melancholy mood of death had taken hold of him. He no longer felt the prickle of drying mud on his skin. It was only death, and his old father lying there on the threshold of the beyond. He shivered and looked again at the composed face. He was not dead. But what were those sightless eyes discerning? What was that far strange look on his face? Wonder?

Juliano could find no fear in his father's face, study it as he would. But was it not a terrible thing to die? Nothing like the fear he had seen there many times in life when the land was dry and grasshoppers sang drily in the fields and the water in the ditch was a mere dampness under the cottonwoods; or when black thunderheads swept down the mountainsides threatening to engulf their little valley and its narrow floor neatly patterned in rectangles of green fields, and lightning roared and echoed in the hollows of the hills. Juliano knew well the look of fear that used to cover old Pablo's face like a mask, but it was not there now.

The son, with a lingering, kindly glance at the dying father, went outside and sat on his haunches beside the house door, leaning his back against the warm adobe wall. For the first time he saw the land as a tyrant bestriding the lives of men, ruling their destinies. It was a frightening thing.

As his eyes roved along the opposing hillsides he saw the stunted junipers which dotted them not as trees but as corporeal imps encircling him like a ring of chattering coyotes. He closed his eyes and felt a burning in them, and all at once he was small and weak and insignificant, as the mantle of old Pablo's responsibility, slipping from the dying shoulders, descended inevitably upon him the oldest son. He realized that nobody had ever made a decision without first consulting the patriarch, and then it had been his decision and not the petitioner's. How could he, Juliano, encompassed by the tyrant land, the heat, the aridity, the convulsions of flood and drought, hope to beat the foe as old Pablo had done? With his eyes still closed he saw himself as in a dream running like mad along an endless corridor pursued by fiends in the shapes of hills, rocks, crags, shrivelled trees and thorny desert bush.

No, he must gather courage, rout the fiends. When he opened his eyes again the hills were in their places, the good water tinkled in the ditch beside him and the land was fair.

Over the brows of the rimming hills, Juliano knew, were more like them, with little valleys between, like their valley, some watered by thin streams from the high mountains shouldering up in the east. From high places the country looked like the wrinkled skin of an old woman, hiding in its folds a few fertile fields. No one would dream of settlements in these crinkly, arid, tree-studded hills; threading a winding way among them the traveller came upon little farming communities with surprise and relief. Far to the west the land levelled off to the *Rio Grande,* where luckier people had wide, well-watered farms and money to spend.

Juliano shrugged and roused himself. No, the world was not as lonely and bitter as it seemed. Men had friends and wiles to battle the land. Beyond that a man couldn't expect much—God's will be done.

He went into the house to ask his wife to call him if any change came over the old father. He found her with the other women in the sick man's room, seated with them along the wall, weeping quietly. The woman beside her was nursing an infant; one great breast shone against her black shawl like a luminous globe in the dim light. Juliano tiptoed to his wife. "Call me if he—wants anything," he whispered, and withdrew.

As he walked down the knoll where the house squatted like a great lump of the tawny earth of which it was made, Juliano thought no more about his father. About that Rosa, rather, his wife. A glimpse of Rosa, such as the one just now, was often enough to set him off on a searching of his heart to find out what it was he felt about her. Jealous, fierce, savage, consuming love, yes, but what else?

He found her there weeping, but he knew she wasn't weeping because she loved the old man. They had never got on well. He always said she was just a kitten, wanting to be kept warm and well fed—not caring much who did the warming and the feeding. And he made no secret of it, either. Rosa knew well enough what he thought of her. She didn't care.

Juliano shook his head, walking slowly down the lane. Old Pablo was wrong about her, though. Juliano had seen more than once how deep she was. That time when he was sick Rosa had taken charge of everything when everybody else was standing around and wailing. And then, too, some of the things she said when they were alone together, in a certain mood of hers when she got deeply quiet and thoughtful, left him hanging on her words like a man dangling from a cloud. Things about love and men and women. Did he love her more than she loved him? Sometimes it seemed so, and it always gave him a pang to think of it. For it made him feel less than Rosa, somehow; made him suffer, too, with a nameless, unremitting ache, as if the one who loves most must suffer most, by some law of life. Rosa herself had said it, not long ago. It was one of those things of such wisdom that, coming from a head so impudent and airy, made him gasp and wonder.

Juliano stopped to rest, leaning his arms on the top rail of the gate letting into the valley road. His head was aswim with thoughts of Rosa, all of them fogged with a strange unclarity. He was suspicious of her, too, wasn't he? With other men? Oh how she could fling him into a seething, tortured agony of jealousy, merely by smiling at a man in a certain way! She knew the way, too, the witch! She knew how to make him suffer. Why did she take such pleasure in it? Can a woman love a man whom she delights to hurt? And how did she know so much, that slender little twig of a girl? What magic? . . .

Juliano shook himself free of this mood, opened the gate and strode down to the field where his brothers were working. Summoning them with a wave of his arm, he told them some of the things the father had said.

"He's pretty bad—he'll die some time to-night, I think."

"Too bad," breathed the brothers almost with one voice, not because they were indifferent, but because they had been taught by a tyrant land to accept death and like disasters in such a spirit. And die he must, every man of them, sooner or later. When a man is old and useless, it is best for him to die, and make room for those coming on.

Only Cruz, the youngest of the three, betrayed a little fear and horror. It showed in his eyes.

"What does he mean", asked this Cruz with a frightened look "when he says we should farm all the land together? That's what we're doing, isn't it?"

"Simple one," said Juliano shortly, "he means just that. We must keep on with it. Don't you see? Look what has already happened in the valley—— When the old men die the boys take the land and split it up into little pieces. Now none of them can make a living off their pieces. We will keep it all together and farm it as one farm—and share in the crop. Don't you see?"

Cruz nodded, silenced. It was good sense all right, but he had a dream of a place of his own when he should marry, and a house of his own, too. He said nothing of it now, for it was not the time. As the youngest, he knew that he would always come last in any family matter. He buried his discontent. "Have you sent for the priest?" he said.

"Yes, he'll be here soon."

It was hot where they were standing, in the middle of the cornfield, although their feet were sunk in the cool mud. "Let's go over to the willows and rest a while," suggested Beatriz, the middle one. "We can talk over there, too."

In the shade of the bushes which lined the banks of the stream, dry now, with all the water in the ditches, they sat down, sticking their legs into the sun's warmth.

16

"You know that old gun of his?" Juliano said, and they nodded. "He gave that to me. He said he wants me to have it."

The other boys chuckled, and Beatriz said: "It's not good for anything. You can't even buy cartridges for it any more. He's had it for fifty years."

"I looked at it just now when I was up at the house. He keeps it on the wall over his bed, you know? It has three more shells."

The brothers laughed gently over the old man's whim. "He thinks it's the greatest gun in the world," said Cruz.

"He thinks it can't miss," Beatriz added. "He's funny about that, remember? He always used to say that he never missed anything with that old rifle."

"I don't think he's shot it for ten years."

"He keeps it clean, though—always ready. The shells he keeps in a little salt sack, tied to the trigger-guard."

They laughed again, softly, reminiscently.

"What did he say about the other things—the house and furniture and——" Cruz looked anxious as he spoke, fearful of being done out of his share.

"He said we should divide all that equally," Juliano explained. "But I don't see how we're going to divide up the house, unless we add some rooms to it."

"We could do that," said Beatriz, "this summer. There's water enough to make adobes still."

"Yes, we could do that."

"We ought to dig a well, too. Remember when we were so sick that time? The doctor said it was from drinking the ditch water."

"Yes, we ought to dig a well."

"Well, after the old man dies, we can make some changes. He never liked changes very much. Look there! The water's running into the road. Come on, we can't waste it like that."

The three brothers leapt to their feet and dashed across the field, spades aloft in their hands.

CHAPTER II

WHEN they looked into old Pablo's will, an informal
document written in Spanish, they were confused,
for the land was described haphazardly; borders and
corners were designated by landmarks no longer
there, and household goods were mentioned and distributed which no longer existed. In the end the
brothers agreed to scrap the will and divide his pos-
sessions as equally as they could. All but Cruz. Cruz
was distrustful of the plan. Throughout the discus-
sions he was a dissenting minority, but as a single
man and little more than a boy, his voice was small
and without weight. Beatriz was married, too, though
only recently, and all of them lived together in
Pablo's house of four rooms. Beatriz and his wife had
one room, Juliano, his wife and two children had two
rooms, and Cruz, when the others were not using it,
had a room of his own, which was also the family
kitchen. It contained, in addition to the cook-stove,
a wide, iron bed, painted white and always immaculately laid with a neat white coverlet. Within the
house, therefore, Cruz had little privacy, and this he

didn't mind in the summer when he could be outside all day and do his dreaming in the cool shade of the cottonwoods which, nurtured by the ancient ditch, spread a canopy over the house and *placita*; but in the winter it was harder to bear. Cruz bided his time and dreamt of the day when he should leave the place and start one of his own. How, without money to buy land, he did not know, but his dreams were never stinted by their frailty.

After the burial of Pablo—it had been one of the greatest wakes the valley had ever seen—the brothers set themselves to the task of making the changes they talked about that day under the willows, when the old father was dying. Juliano chose a spot in the *placita* for a well, and Cruz and his brother Beatriz started making adobes. It was in the back of the youngest boy's head, when the time came, to advocate the building of a new house altogether apart from the old place, hard by a grove of elders and cottonwoods down the valley from there. He hoped one day to have it for his own, though he knew that one of the married brothers would want it first, in any case. At least it would give more room in the old house, to get one of the families out of there.

A new air about the place was evident since the old man's passing. A new bustle and activity. Even the women felt it and manifested it in the busy way they went about their work and talked of plans and changes. Rosa started a vegetable garden in a patch of watered ground below the house, and told how she intended to put up enough vegetables in jars to last all winter. Other women in the valley did, why shouldn't she? The old man had always been against it because he said it couldn't be done. And when she spoke of old Pablo, now that he was gone, it was not with reverence for his memory, but with relief at his passing. Juliano saw this, and it hurt him. Yet it was no good being hurt by it. It was over and done with. The old man had never liked her, anyway——

It had taken root in Juliano, what the old man had thought of Rosa, enough to worry him—but not enough to make him believe any of it. He loved her. He was proud that this handsomest girl in the valley had chosen him, out of a number of possible husbands, including one Ben Ortiz, who had been foraging for a wife at the same time. Yes, he loved her and he intended to keep her. He'd never let her go. She had a wandering eye—Juliano could see that without half looking—but it had caused no trouble yet, and he thought he almost had her tamed, with two children and a house to look after. And still when he thought of Rosa he felt a gush of warmth go through him. That was a sign that he loved her, wasn't it? It was like stepping from the shade into the warm sunlight, when he thought of Rosa.

His brothers wasted little love on her, though.

They all got on well enough, living in the same house and all, but quarrels came up now and again which formerly the old man had always settled, with an imperious word or two. He was an old tyrant, all right, but no doubt good for them. It remained to be seen how they would get along without him.

Juliano was digging the well now, in his spare time from the fields. Between sundown and darkness he could be heard but not seen out there in the *placita*, with nothing to tell his whereabouts except rhythmic spurts of dirt out of the hole in the ground where he was working. He was down about ten feet, and the earth at the bottom of the well was still as dry as powder.

Grimy and covered with sweat, he climbed out of the hole when he could no longer see down there, and went in to supper, of green vegetables and green chilli in addition to the usual beans and *tortillas*. With work to do and good food to eat, a man couldn't complain in the summer.

Every Saturday night the people of the valley fore-gathered in a big bare barn of a place near the church and had a dance. Ben Ortiz was the fiddler, but he liked to dance, too, and half the time he was down off the platform, cavorting around the room with the girls. He was a popular dancer, and a gay fellow. People said Rosa would have married him after Juliano, and some even wondered why she hadn't married him in the first place. Juliano was so serious beside Ben. Not any better, either, they said. Ben had a good farm, inherited from his father, and a good, steady way with him. He and Juliano had grown up together and had been friends through their childhood; but the rivalry over Rosa had put a thing between them that hadn't yet dissolved. They eyed each other without love.

Both protested that they had nothing against the other, and why not be friends? Yet they remained aloof, not daring or caring to make the first friendly overture. Juliano still distrusted Ben. It was no secret that Rosa still liked him. Anybody could see that; the way they danced together on Saturday nights, and disappeared outside for quick walks in the hills, and came back looking guilty. These incidents set fire to Juliano, because he could do nothing about them. They were innocent, as far as he could tell or guess. Rosa only laughed when he complained.

"Do you want me to be like a burro, always staying home? You dance with other girls. You kiss other girls in the moonlight. Why shouldn't I have some fun?"

"Does he make love to you?" Juliano would ask darkly.

And Rosa would give him a ripple of laughter. "Why, of course not. I don't let him do *that*."

"How do I know you don't?"

23

Then she would get angry. He couldn't abide her anger—it frightened him and made him afraid of losing her. "Because I tell you so," she would shout at him.

Beaten, Juliano would hold his tongue; but the wrath at Ben would not be appeased.

Well, it was only on Saturday nights and Sunday mornings. For the rest of the week they were all so busy that they hadn't time to fuss about jealousies and quarrels. Juliano came to a ledge of rock at the bottom of his well and had to stop. And nothing really mattered as long as the tyrant land left them in peace. While water flowed in the ditch and the corn grew and the alfalfa waved green plumes in the breeze, a man could look upon these sights and be consoled.

Cruz and Beatriz had about two thousand adobes made. When Juliano consulted them about his problem in the well, they put their heads together and decided to go to the town for dynamite. With an army post there, and big stores like the Spengelburg's, explosives must be available. Yes, they'd have to get somebody out to set it off—they didn't know how to do it, might blow up the whole place in trying. They'd need some money, too, but that wasn't so difficult. They'd take a day off and cut wood, load up a dozen burros and sell it in the town. With twelve loaded burros they could make the twelve miles into town in a day, and come back the next.

The plan was settled. Juliano thought and thought about it, they discussed it at all the meals, and the women had their say as well. Rosa laughed at them, journeying cautiously home with a load of dynamite on a burro, and what would they do if the little beast should fall down and blow his brains out? They didn't share her amusement. The two younger brothers were short with her, accused her of always laughing at the wrong time, at the wrong thing. Juliano was embarrassed and tried weakly to laugh with her. And he wondered why she seemed so gay at the thought of their going.

He brooded about it, scolded his children and made himself generally disagreeable. Yet he could find no good reason in his heart for his feelings. He didn't want to leave her alone for so long, and he pretended to his brothers that he was anxious for her and the children, alone on the place without a man around; and he tried to persuade one of his brothers to stay home. They made light of his fears. What could possibly happen, with neighbours within shouting distance, in midsummer when it was warm and life was easy? Besides, they all felt the need of a holiday in the town, and wouldn't pass up the chance for any silly fears of Juliano's.

Then he tried to make Rosa say she'd come to town with them, and again she only laughed. Why

should she go in with them? What had she to gain
by sitting idly for two days on the seat of a wagon?
If she didn't go they wouldn't have to take a wagon
at all—they could ride the burros one way, at least,
and she wouldn't ride a burro all that distance for
no reason at all except a notion of her husband.

Juliano gave up, and went out with his brothers to
cut wood.

It was hot work. All the time he was working,
Juliano thought about himself and Rosa and Ben
Ortiz. He's better-looking than I am, he thought; he
laughs more and makes jokes all the time. He makes
the girls laugh. He always did. They always liked
him better than me; I thought for a long time that
Rosa would marry him instead of me. I still don't
know why she didn't. Maybe she thought I had a
better farm. Maybe she thought I'd take better care
of her—give her more things. How much do women
think about such things when they get married?
More than a man does?

He never thought about anything except how
beautiful Rosa was, and how blissful to have her in
his bed. Oh, these women! When they're not teasing
a man like a she-dog, they're scheming some way to
get something out of him, or to deceive him about
something.

He drove his axe into the trunk of a juniper tree
with a cleaving smash as if it were the head of an

26

enemy, and he got pleasure from the cleanness of the blow. A man could end all his troubles by treating his woman like that. Ah, but then he wouldn't have her, and he'd have to lie alone at night. *Por Dios*, a man was caught between the devil and the dead! His peace was ruined by one thing or another. He should marry a cow of a woman, but he'd soon grow tired of her, then. No, there was nothing for it. He'd have to go to town and leave her to do as she would. But if she tried anything with that Ben Ortiz, he'd use his axe on one or both of them. He'd warn her of that, anyway, before he left, as God was good!

As God was good. So they said; so it must be. God had given him this woman to keep, and keep her he must, for good or ill. No escaping that.

When Juliano came home from the woodcutting, he was tired and ill-tempered. He looked searchingly at Rosa, busy in the kitchen.

"What have you been doing to-day?" he asked gruffly, as if she hadn't been working the whole time. He didn't wait for her reply which he knew would be flippant, and turned to Nina, the wife of Beatriz. "Has she been behaving herself, Nina?"

"Oh, *si*, Juliano, she has. We've been here all day."

"What did you think I've been doing, dancing with Ben Ortiz?" Rosa taunted.

Juliano went outside. He had perforce to think of Nina compared to his Rosa. She was a dull girl. He sat down beside the hole in the ground which one day, God and American dynamite willing, would be their well. He picked up a stone and flung it into the hole with all his force. Oh, what made him so ugly? Just because he was tired——

Yes, it was better to have a woman with some spirit, instead of a meek little cow like that Nina. But he went to the door again and beckoned Rosa outside. She came with enough docility to please an ogre.

"What do you want, Juliano? Can't you see I'm busy?"

"Listen to me, Rosa. To-morrow I'm going into the town with the other boys. I'll be gone two days. What will you and Nina do?"

"What will we do? Why, just what we always do, every day. Work, work, work."

Juliano looked long and steadfastly into her eyes. No, by God and the saints, he saw no constancy there. She wasn't a good woman like little Nina. She had an itch for the men, it smouldered in her eyes—laughing eyes. If their laughter should ever be turned on him——

"I want you to promise me to be good while I'm gone," he said, feeling stupid saying it. Words would never stop her. "I want you to stay here on the place and—and look after the stock, and——"

Oh, what was the good of inventing reasons? She

knew what was in his mind—those damnable laughing eyes. He flew into a useless rage. "If I catch you with that Ben Ortiz while I'm gone, I'll kill you both!"

"Oh, Juliano," she cried with mock fright. Then, slyly: "How can you catch me—while you're gone?"

Juliano cursed under his breath and went into the house. Her rippling laughter followed him, tormentingly.

CHAPTER III

EVERYBODY in the valley—the settlement contained only about a dozen families, all related more or less closely now after three hundred years—heard about the plan of the Trujillo brothers, Cruz and Beatriz and Juliano, to blow the bottom out of their well. They were foolish to dig it just there, so high above the floor of the valley, but those Trujillos thought they knew everything. Old Pablo had made them think so, because he was the most respected man in the valley while he lived. The sage of the countryside. Now, with the old man gone, they watched the brothers with amusement, awaiting the irony of their fall.

Dynamite was risky stuff, almost unknown in the community. They had no use for it, really—the bottom land had all been cleared long, long ago by their forefathers. If a man was fool enough to dig a well through rock, of course he'd have to use something beside his bare hands.

They laughed at the Trujillos. And Ben Ortiz laughed with them. He had a well, but it was down near the creek, and his wife brought water from it in buckets. Were the Trujillos so grand that their women couldn't walk a hundred feet to water? A couple of days' work on the Ortiz well, and they had all the water they needed.

Ben Ortiz heard also about the projected trip of the brothers to the town, and when he heard of it his heart beat faster of its own accord. Nothing in the news should make his heart beat faster; he didn't care whether they went to town or not. Oh, didn't he?

Damn that woman!

In going, they would have to pass along the road near his house. And on the day chosen he didn't go to work in his fields until he saw the lazy caravan moving by, the burros picking their way daintily like maidens at a dance, and all but hidden by their loads of wood. He watched them file up the winding road out of the valley, and when the last lean figure vanished over the brow of the hill, he stood up and stretched himself and rubbed his hands together.

Ben Ortiz affected a little moustache. He laughingly explained it by saying that it tickled the girls when he kissed them and they liked it. The real reason was that it hurt his skin to shave his upper lip, so he left the hair on it. And it did give him an air. With his tall, lean frame and regular features, it added just the culminating touch of distinction. Other men in the valley were plain beside Ben Ortiz, and he knew it. Then, too, his blood was not thin. His mother came from another place, so that the fluid which flowed in Ben's veins was not strained for a hundred years through the same sieve.

He treated his wife like a good mare. He was proud of her, and as tender as he would be with a good brood mare. She bore him a child every year, until this year when something had happened. They had three children, a boy and two girls—good, sturdy kids who knew their place. But a brood mare was not much fun, and Ben had lusty appetites.

When he saw the Trujillo caravan disappearing over the brow of the hill, he smiled and rubbed his hands together. Before an old broken mirror in the kitchen he shaped the ends of his moustache and brushed his shirt, deciding in the end to put on a clean one. No, on second thought, he'd wait until the morning's work was done and put one on after dinner, and take a walk down the valley road to see how things were going with his neighbours. On the way down to his fields he sang a gay Spanish tune. He, with Cruz Trujillo and some others, was one of a group who met often to sing and serenade on summer evenings. He did all his work alone, except in harvest and sowing times, when it was customary for everybody to turn in and help his friends. Ben had no brothers living with him to complicate his life, either —he was his own master.

Rosa felt an adventurous lift of her heart also when the men departed. She had no plans—it was just that she savoured the freedom of being left alone with Nina. Nina was easy to manage; she could make the meek little wife of Beatriz do anything she wanted her to do, she could close her eyes or her ears or her mouth with a word. She could send her packing off on some innocent errand if need be. Nina was easily managed. Her place in the household was even lower than that of Cruz, the youngest—she would even take orders from Cruz. All the meanest tasks were left for Nina. Between them they kept the house spotlessly clean, the walls immaculately white.

Rosa sang as she washed the breakfast dishes—or dried them, rather. Nina did the washing. And when she got her children dressed she turned them loose in the *placita* and forgot about them. They never worried Rosa, once they were out of the house on a summer day, for the *placita* was bountiful with amusement for a child, and they had the world of the valley to roam in, and they looked after one another. The dry hole of Juliano's well was their delight just now; José, the oldest one, was big enough to get down the ladder into the dark chill depths of the hole, and it was enough for the younger one to watch him climb in and out and wonder at his fortitude. The thought that one of them might topple into the thing never occurred to Rosa, though she loved José with a fierce possessiveness.

She finished the work inside the house and went down to her garden patch for a while to hoe the weeds. She put on a clean dress. She didn't work very hard. She could look up and see Nina washing clothes in a tub beside the ditch, and she smiled at the innocence of little Nina, working so hard for no good reason. When Beatriz came back she would point out to him all the work she had done, and if he patted her gently she would feel repaid. Rosa smiled somewhat crookedly.

She soon tired of working there in the hot sun, and sat down in the shade of a giant cottonwood growing at the edge of the little field. The grass was lush and green under it because, whenever the garden patch was irrigated, the water came down that way in a little waterfall at the base of the big tree.

Rosa looked up through the branches to the sky. The under sides of the leaves were silver, quaking in the soft breeze like jewels, and the sky beyond was deep, deep blue, inviting dreams. Rosa stretched out and put her arms under her head. She felt a vibratory unity with the earth, her body was one with the earth-body in some mysterious way. Arching her back, she flaunted the rich curves of her breasts to the sky, as if it were a human lover. Oh, it was good to be young and full of desire! She closed her eyes and thought of

34

Juliano, trudging along the road behind those sleepy burros, mile after dusty mile. And she smiled. What things men will do, all because their funny little wills are forever building, building, like children with mud blocks. Funny, funny little men. Did she love Juliano, she asked herself luxuriously? Oh, yes. In a way. He was fun to tease, and he was a good man—a very good man. Faithful, hard-working, earnest. But, heaven! there were other men in the world. Other men who were different, and knew how to give a woman some fun. For a husband a woman wanted a good steady man like Juliano—what a woman really needed was two or three husbands, but the fools wouldn't allow that. Oh, no. They must have one woman, and he must be enough for her.

Well, what if he wasn't enough? She sat up rebelliously. They thought they had a woman beaten, didn't they? With their laws and their customs and jealousies. Well, let them think so. But they were wrong.

A new thought entered Rosa's head. She looked once more into the sky. To the east, over the high mountains a vast slate-grey thunderhead was massing, rearing in titanic curves for an assault upon the earth. It would rain later. Now would be the time for a stroll along the valley road, to see how things were with the neighbours before the storm.

She jumped to her feet and straightened her dress.

Then she picked a long spear of wild grass and chewed the end of it. Putting on her shoes, which she had kicked off when she started to hoe the rows of cabbages, she sauntered down the lane leading to the valley road, where she turned upstream. The sunlight gleamed in her blue-black hair, and the laughter danced in her eyes.

Ben Ortiz saw her leaning against the fence which separated his field from the valley road, when he looked up from hoeing. And his heart gave a bound. He didn't expect her to come to him like this—it was a rare thing. He pushed his hat back from his sweating forehead, threw down his hoe and walked over to her with a swagger.

Through Ben's eyes this Rosa was a mystery. Hot and cold by turns, moody as a cloudy summer day. A man never knew where he stood with her at all. Sometimes the look in her eyes took his heart and twisted it like a rag, and again the brittle chill in them made him recoil. He spent all his time with her wondering what her mood was now, and when he thought he had found out, it changed again.

To-day, as he searched her face which just cleared the topmost wire on the fence, he could see nothing in it except plain flirtatiousness. And his heart quickened. It was the mood he liked best, understood best. It was all easy and outgoing, and made no demands on him other than simple physical

36

demands which he could eloquently satisfy. She bared her white teeth and cocked her black eyes as she chewed on the tip of a piece of grass. Her head, never centred soberly, was always tipped on one side or the other, and her eyelashes, when she dropped her gaze from his face, swept their curving length along her cheeks. And Ben stared at her with his mouth slightly open, like a man transfixed by a vision.

After watching her for a long time his face broadened in a grin, showing his own gleaming teeth.

"Well, Rosa. I'm surprised to see you here now—in the morning. Everybody's got work to do in the mornings, no?"

"Oh, I finished my work," she said shortly. "Nina helps."

Ben had his two big fists closed around the top fence-wire, between the barbs. Now in his nervous unclosing of his hands he moved them and pricked himself on a barb. Rosa's eyes opened wide for a moment when he yelped over the pain of it, and this didn't escape him. She cared for him then? She was sorry he hurt his hand. He sucked blood from the scratch. He had to watch every second of his time with Rosa; nothing was without significance, every look, breath, motion, meant something. And yet he never managed to anticipate her, she was so quick and changeable.

37

Conversation languished between them this morning, as Rosa stood there by the fence shifting her weight from one foot to the other, tipping her head from side to side and archly chewing the piece of grass. But this was the language Ben knew best, and he wasn't bothered by the lack of words.

"Where are you going?"

Rosa lifted her shapely shoulders in a shrug. "Oh—just for a little walk."

"A little walk," he repeated. "Well—looks like it may rain later."

Rosa gave him one of her most inviting smiles because she felt disposed to Ben, and this was the way he liked her best. Ben was as easy as a child. All she had to do was smile and wave her hips at him. Most men were pretty easy, for that matter, once a girl found out what they liked, where their foolish self-importance could be touched. And it gave Rosa a lift to use her power over them and to see them tumble like little targets before her fire. But when familiarity bred tough defences in them, it was no longer any fun. That was the trouble with Juliano. He was practically immune to her now, though he loved her when he thought of it.

Ben still responded like a puppy. He was fun.

She looked up at the sky and saw a great cloud rolling over the mountains. "Yes, it might rain," she said. "It's all right. We need it."

Ben nodded. "We always need it. If it rained every day it wouldn't be too much."

The talk means nothing, Ben was telling himself. But pretty soon he'd have to pin her down to something or she'd get away again, as she always had in the past. She advanced to the threshold of a man's desire and bounded away, leaving him panting and often mad. Some day, Ben had said, he'd get her and make her give what she promised so freely. And this —who knows?—might be the time, with Juliano and all the men away. He looked up at the sky again.

"Looks like a big cloud, Rosa. Maybe Juliano will get wet, no?"

Rosa was startled for a moment. "You know?——"

And Ben grinned with the pleasure of his advantage. "Sure, I saw them go by. Beatriz, Cruz and Juliano," he counted them off triumphantly.

Rosa shrugged, and lowered her eyes. She was still chewing on the spear of grass.

Ben felt the stirring of a quick desire, and knew that he had every right to it. She came here of her own accord, she rolled her eyes and swayed her hips at him. What more signal could a man require? And what kind of a man would ignore it?

"What are you going to do—all day?" he said.

"Oh, I don't know."

"Who's at the house?"

"Only Nina—and the children."

39

"Well——" Ben hesitated. "I'll be through here in a little while. Why don't you wait, and—and I'll walk back with you?"

"No. I've got to go now."

"Will you come back?"

"Maybe."

Rosa strolled away, but not towards her house. And Ben stood a moment watching her, a smile playing about his lips. He went back to work, but kept an eye on the valley road. His heart refused to quiet down, and he cursed himself. What was it about that woman that made a man stir just to lay his eyes on her? It had always been so. He didn't like her especially—certainly he wasn't in love with her. Married to a woman like that a man would have no peace at all. He'd be forever wondering what she was up to, and before long he'd come to hate the sight of her because he couldn't trust her. But her beauty would keep him going so he couldn't throw her out or let her go.

Ben shook his head over his hoe. No, he wanted only one thing of a woman like Rosa—and it looked as if he would get it.

He saw her coming and ran down to the fence to intercept her. This time he climbed over it and met her in the road.

"Come along, Rosa—I'll walk with you a little way."

She said nothing, but fell in beside him and walked on.

"Where shall we go?" said Ben.

"Oh—let's go down by the river. It's nice and cool down there."

Ben's heart increased. The willows and elders made a thick screen along the stream's edge and choked the banks with undergrowth. Occasional open spaces were obscured from all but the sky. "All right," he agreed. "We can get down through the gate here, across my field."

Rosa had another piece of grass in her teeth. Now and then she brushed against Ben, as if by accident. And Ben held on to himself, doubtful of what he seemed to see. But there was no doubt about what he was feeling. No doubt at all.

When they came to the first barrier of densely growing bushes, Ben charged and forced an opening for them. In a moment, as the branches closed in behind them they were concealed as utterly as if they had vanished from the earth. Overhead the sky was blue, with great clouds curling. They walked in the dry bed of the stream for a while, Rosa leading, Ben following her grimly, more like a man stalking an animal. Now he had to think of Juliano—for all his making fun of him, Ben liked Juliano. Hadn't they grown up together, herded sheep together, run, slept, played together? With a shade of difference in the circumstances, he would have taken this little witch and slapped her provocative behind and sent her home.

She ran ahead and disappeared from his vision around a turning in the river-bed—and Ben paused for a moment's consideration. What should he do? After all, it was no responsibility of his. She came to him, she was a lovely woman offering herself unmistakably. What kind of a man would turn his back on a thing like that? The valley was not so big that a girl as lush as Rosa could be had every day.

No, it was no fault of his; with a grunt he threw off his doubts and broke into a run. He found her in one of those open places ringed about by willows, and she was lying down on her back and one knee was flexed in a way that showed more of her legs than was accidental.

"Come and lie here, Ben—it's so soft on the grass."

Ben needed no invitation now. He sat down on the ground beside her. The grass was cool between his fingers. Grass was such a luxury in the barren land that a man relished it. Even now Ben thought how good it was, and he looked down seriously into Rosa's eyes.

"Rosa, Rosa, do you know what you are doing?"

For answer she arched the full curves of her breasts to him, as she had done earlier to the sky. Oh, this was better than the cold, austere, far sky!

But she said: "Do you think I'm a child, Ben?"

And Ben said: "I don't know," and fell upon her hungrily.

She let his searching hands go where they would, but she was on her guard. When he was about to subdue her she whimpered and cried out and frightened him. What was this? Three times, inflamed to a madness of lust for her, Ben had to hesitate because of her cries, and the third time she slipped from his arms and sat a little apart from him.

And suddenly she was as pensive as she had been reckless before. Ben could only gape at her in his astonishment, and scratch his head.

"No, no, Ben. Wait. Not now. Not now."

"What's the matter, Rosa? A minute ago you were——"

She turned wide eyes to him. "I feel—I feel different all of a sudden. The sky is so blue, and the birds —hear how they sing! Oh, the earth is beautiful, Ben! Isn't it?"

Ben scratched his head, or rather continued to scratch it. "But, Rosa——"

"Listen, Ben. Sometimes when I'm alone I dream, even in the daytime. I don't have to be asleep to dream. Do you?"

"Why, sure, I——"

"And I dream", she hurried on as if Ben were not there at all, "of things that never happen, people and

43

places that never were—couldn't be. Ben——" she turned on him suddenly. "Ben, you'll be nice to me, won't you? Sometime?"

"Of course, Rosa. If you'll only give me a chance."

"I'll give you a chance!"

"When?"

"Oh, to-night, maybe. You ask too many questions, Ben." And she gave him a mocking laugh.

He grasped her by the wrists and held her in his rigid arms. "It will be to-night, then, Rosa. And no more fooling."

She laughed and was serious again without answering him. But assent enough stood in her eyes, and he let her go. "Ben," she said with such a frown that he thought she was going to scold him, "before you were married, did you ever think of marriage and—and what it would be like?"

"Oh, I guess I did." But he was still full of the torment of thwarted lust and reached for her across the intervening green space.

Rosa drew away from him. "No, no, Ben. I used to think it would be wonderful to be married." Her eyes were half-closed and she picked another piece of grass to nibble on. "I never had any fun before ——" she narrowed her eyes still more and lifted a corner of her upper lip in a kind of pretty snarl. "They kept me chained up, like a dog. I wasn't allowed to go out alone, ever, or look at a man. I

44

hardly ever saw the moon except through a window of our house. The moon is pretty to look at, don't you think so, Ben?"

Ben gave a grunt, more expressive of his impatience than of any love for the moon. He was already bored with all this fine talk.

"I thought it would be wonderful to have a man to love me all the time," Rosa went on dreamily, biting the end of her piece of grass. "But—I guess men don't love—like that. Do they?" She turned her big eyes on him with that, and Ben groped in a black confusion.

"Well, I don't know, Rosa. Men are all different. Maybe you'd find one some day, somewhere, who'd be like that."

And Rosa smiled, lifting the cloud at once from Ben's mind. He could understand her when she smiled. "Would you love me always, Ben, if we were married? Would you come to me whenever I called, and kiss me every time I wanted to be kissed?"

Taking this to be another invitation, Ben reached for her again across the sward, and was rebuffed as before. He retired in perplexity. What kind of a woman was this Rosa, anyway? Was she playing with him, teasing him, like a cat with a mouse? He began to be angry. He had no time to waste on a mood like this. He stood up. "Well, I've got to be going, Rosa. I've got water running into my wheat."

Rosa didn't move, didn't even look up to him. "All right, Ben. Good-bye."

His voice was ominous, though, when he said: "I'll see you later, Rosa. I'm coming up to your house to-night. You said——"

And Rosa, changing again like a wisp of smoke, laughed back to him, tipped her head to one shoulder and cried airily: "Will you be nice to me, Ben—sometime?"

Ben stood looking at her half angrily, half joyfully —and with a wild shake of his head he was off through the underbrush.

When he had gone, Rosa stretched out full length on the precious grass. Was she happy now? Was this thing, that made her heart sing, happiness? And if so, what was that other sadness lying just beneath? Was it the root of happiness, dark, sombre, like the roots of a tree under the earth? Her heart was brimming, was it not, with love of life and Ben Ortiz? Then why this heavy feeling around her heart, enclosing her happiness like a grim stone wall? Why, even now as she thought about him, did she feel a wave of contempt for Ben Ortiz? And a surge of sympathy for Juliano? Whom did she love? Anybody? Only herself? Only Rosa?

Rosa! Ah, that made her feel good again. Rosa was beautiful, Rosa was fair! Rosa had a lovely body and round, firm breasts for a man to hold in his hand.

Mirrors and still waters smiled when Rosa looked into them! The eyes of men shone with quick desire when Rosa spoke to them—yes, even if she scolded them and spat at them like a she-cat. They liked it. They thought it was pretty.

Her laugh sounded merrily along the river-bed, though no one was near to hear. She rolled on the turf like a puppy and rubbed her whole body on the ground. Rosa was beautiful! She was for love, Rosa was, young, beautiful—for love! What else mattered? Nothing. Nothing. Rosa was put on the earth for love! Ben would come, and she would love him, and that would be good.

It was a long time before Ben Ortiz calmed down after his walk with Rosa. He thought of her constantly, his heart filled him with sly romantic pricks at every turn of the day. Was this love he was feeling, then? Well, one thing he knew—she wouldn't get away again. She wouldn't fool him any longer. He'd make her give, make her keep her promises.

All through the midday dinner he sat looking sourly at his wife without speaking, and through the afternoon he cultivated the cornfield in a fever of jumbled thoughts and plans. At nine o'clock in the evening he left his house, telling his wife he was going down the valley to see a friend. She knew better than to ask questions. Perhaps she didn't care. She saw him step out into the moonlight and disappear.

The heat of his passion was still on him, and it was mixed with anger. He was a man of honour, but no woman was going to make a fool of him. She was a little witch, that Rosa was!

At the Trujillo house he advanced cautiously, making no sound, ignoring the barking dog. He tapped softly on the door where he knew Rosa slept. She let him in, showing only mild surprise at his coming.

And this time her cries were less urgent, and deterred him not at all.

CHAPTER IV

JULIANO had no peace on his journey. The physical
discomforts of it only heightened the anxiety he felt
over Rosa and what she might be doing. Thoughts
of her obsessed him, and everything he saw reminded
him of Rosa. It was stimulating to get to the town
and to see its crowded *plaza*, with teams and riding
horses lining the hitch-rails, an occasional lumbering
wagon, and the four-horse stage from the north.
Soldiers in uniform were everywhere, and Indians in
gaudy shirts. And the hot sun pierced the cloud of
dust which hung over the place like a haze. While
Cruz and Beatriz were about the business of buying
dynamite, Juliano, left to stable the burros, wandered
into the cool square in the centre of the *plaza* and sat
down on a bench, shut off from the streets by a
white picket fence.

Another time he might have enjoyed this change;
he might even have used some of the money for
pleasure, got pleasantly drunk after dark, perhaps
found an obliging wench in some saloon. To-day he
had no heart for any of those things.

D   49

When his brothers came back their breath smelled faintly of liquor, and Juliano scowled disapprovingly and urged them to be careful. How much would the dynamite be?

"It costs too much," said Beatriz. "We got black powder instead—just as good."

Juliano nodded. "Maybe it's better. We know how to use black powder. We've got to find a place to sleep to-night."

"We can sleep in the hay down at Umberto's place," Beatriz suggested. "It's warm. No use spending money for a room somewhere."

"How much have we got left?"

"Five American dollars." Beatriz spoke the words incredulously, and held out the silver pieces in the palm of his hand, clinked them together with his fingers.

"Shall we spend it?" said Cruz eagerly. It was only the second time in his life that he had been to town, and the first time he was a child. "We could take some things back. Five dollars—*por Dios!*"

They were standing now on a corner of the *plaza* in the deepening dusk; at their backs the doors of Jake Spengelburg's store opened upon a robbers' cave of exotic goods. In front of them at the intersection of streets an old cannon was stuck into the ground muzzle first to keep wagons from cutting the corner too closely. Juliano leaned wearily against this while they talked. The brothers could see the worried look of him.

"What's the matter, Juliano? Anything wrong? You're not sick, are you?"

"Me, sick? No. I'm not sick. I'm—tired, that's all. It was a long, hot walk to town."

"Well, what shall we do?"

They watched, instead of deciding at once, the scenes on the *plaza*. Dust was still raised by the scuffling feet of horses and the incessant turning of wagon-wheels. But it was quieter now at the day's end. Lamps appeared in some windows and the stores were brilliantly lighted, for it was Saturday night. The brothers, huddled together beside the old cannon, felt like strangers in a foreign land, and though none of them expressed it, each was feeling a nostalgic longing for the silence of Vallecito, the little valley. Thus it had been named literally in the beginning, and so it had remained. Vallecito.

Cruz grew impatient. "Why don't we eat?"

"All right." Juliano roused himself. "Let's eat."

"Where?" said Beatriz.

"Oh, any of these places—wait, I know a place down below where we can get good food." By good food, Juliano meant *chilli con carne*, *tortillas*, and coffee.

"All right."

The brothers left the old cannon and marched three

abreast along one side of the *plaza* and turned down a long, dingy street lined on both sides by saloons.

Juliano nudged his brother Beatriz. "Better put the money somewhere, so they can't find it."

After dinner, they revisited the stables where the burros were, smoked cigarettes for a while. Cruz was restless, Juliano was dour. At last Juliano lay down in the hay and went to sleep. It was too much for Cruz.

"Come on, Beatriz—we don't want to go to sleep yet—do we?"

Beatriz looked kindly at his young brother. "No," he agreed, gently, and fumbled in his belt. "Here, take these two dollars and have some fun. I'm tired."

Cruz grabbed the money and ran.

"Mind you don't get too drunk and land in the jail," Beatriz called after him, and Cruz waved reassuringly from the gate.

"How much did you give him?"

Juliano's voice from the hay startled Beatriz. "I gave him two dollars."

"Too much," growled Juliano. "He'll spend it all. We've got to buy a bucket and rope for the well, and a pulley. Are you crazy?"

"Oh, go to sleep, Juliano. This is his first time in the town. Let him have some fun."

"What about the things we've got to buy?"

"There's more wood in the hills. We can come

again when your well is finished. What's the matter with you? Are you sick?"

"Sick?" Juliano groaned. "Maybe I'm sick in the head." And he rubbed his forehead and eyes with his hands.

"Is it Rosa?"

Juliano looked up at Beatriz, who was standing over him. "What makes you say that?"

Beatriz shrugged. "I just thought it might be."

"And if it is?"

"Forget it."

Juliano rolled over in the hay with his back to Beatriz. Forget it, he said. Forget Rosa? No man could do that. His fingers kept stroking the woollen scarf she had made for him. With her quick, clever hands she had made it. He thought about her hands; by closing his eyes tight he could see them go, as he had watched them many times, sewing or weaving. No hands were as quick and clever as Rosa's. Miraculous hands, swift and sure. She made things in half the time that it took other women, and with half the effort. She could turn out a dress for the babies in an hour or two, and it would be a pretty dress, prettier than other childrens' dresses. Her own clothes, too. How pretty her own clothes were, now that he thought of it. Even when she was hot and tired from cooking and working, Rosa looked neat and pretty.

53

A wonderful thing, that. Seeing her every day, all the time, a man was likely to forget those things about Rosa, how clever she was, and how pretty always. And Juliano reminded himself that it would be well to let her know how he felt about it, and how he remembered such things about her. That was one way a man lost a woman, by forgetting to keep such things in mind, and telling her about them once in a while. If he doesn't, some sly coyote like Ben Ortiz comes along and tells her she's beautiful and clever and makes her think her husband's forgotten her, or doesn't appreciate her.

Juliano stirred restlessly in the hay. Ben Ortiz, the fox—he might be doing just that, right now!

What made her hands so quick? The same thing that made her eyes shine and laugh? They always said of witches that they had quick, sure hands. Oh, sleep, sleep!

When Cruz unsteadily returned to the corral four hours later, he saw the red glow of a cigarette in the hay. It was dangerous to smoke like that in the hay, he thought, and went closer to investigate. It was Juliano, sitting up. "I thought you'd be asleep."

"No. Did you spend all that money, Cruz?"

"No."

"How much have you got left?"

"I don't know. You count it." Cruz produced some coins and passed them to Juliano, who grunted.

54

"Fifteen cents. Is that all?"

But Cruz was already asleep in the hay.

In the morning they bought a bucket—a fine, oaken bucket with steel bands around it—a pulley, and some things for the wives. And the long journey home began. Before an hour had passed Cruz climbed on to one of the burros and sat there drooping, swaying jerkily to the mincing steps of the little beast. Juliano walked in silence, his black eyes focused on the distance, unseeing. Off and on they rode one or another of the burros, and before they started up into the hills where Vallecito lay hidden, they made Cruz get off and change to a different one.

He rode with eyes shut against the tyrant land. The characteristic pink hills, spotted with the dark green of stumpy trees. How the relentless sun beat down from above and the sharp, horny land from below! And the dust rose to stifle them and the hills to test their strength. And the little burros, indifferent, stifflegged, plodded on.

Beatriz was the only one of the three who noticed the land. Cruz was too far gone in drowsiness, and Juliano in the dark recesses of his thoughts. It was Beatriz who looked back now and again from the high places in the hills and gazed with wonder at the vast bowl of shimmering land behind them and the vaster bowl of limitless blue above. He felt tiny, like a mote suspended in a bubble. Huge, huge, this land of theirs. A man was nothing in it. What could his puny efforts forfend? How could it matter what befell?

Poor Juliano! who had a sly she-fox for a wife, for good or ill. What could it matter to the earth or sky? To the mountains or the hills or the grey curling clouds? God's will be done. God's will be done.

But when they topped the last hill and dipped into the warm intimacy of their little valley, all, including the burros, came alive again. Juliano's eyes swept the valley road and searched along the flat, grass-grown roofs and among the shadows of the cottonwoods. The good smell of moist earth and water in a thirsty land! The sound of some boys singing came to them brokenly on the wayward air. Even Cruz sat erect on his burro and opened his eyes. Conversation began.

"What did you do last night, Cruz, that makes you so sleepy?"

And Cruz grinned at his brother Beatriz.

"Was she pretty, Cruz? Was she nice?"

Cruz could only grin again, while Beatriz laughed. But Juliano would not be roused to a smile, out of the caverns of his thought. His face remained set and hard, and the brothers left him alone, noticing, when they passed the house of Ben Ortiz, how he turned dark looks upon the place.

All was peace at the Trujillo home. The women rushed out to meet them, Nina flying into the arms of Beatriz, Rosa sauntering down the lane with a nonchalant swaying of her hips. And Juliano went to her and took both her hands and stared into her eyes, looking for something there, while his two boys pulled at his trouser-legs for attention. Then he kissed her, hard.

"Did you have a good time? Was it a hot trip? How was it in town? And Cruz, what happened to *you?*"

When the burros had been unloaded and turned out to graze they all went into the house, gathering in the kitchen which was also Cruz's room, and small gifts were distributed to the two wives. Beatriz had a new black shawl for Nina, and Juliano gave Rosa a cotton dress. Rosa held it to her shoulders and asked them how it looked, and Nina cried for joy. Cruz felt left out of it, and yearned for a wife, although he wanted no more of women for a while. Lying down on the bed, he was soon loudly asleep, and they laughed at him.

"No rain here?" Juliano asked when he was able to get Rosa alone.

"No. I thought it would rain yesterday, but the clouds passed by. And you? Did it rain on you?"

"No. What did you do, Rosa? Were you lonely without us?"

"Yes—but we were busy all the time. Nina did all the washing, and I weeded the vegetables. It wasn't so bad."

"Did anybody come to see you?"

"No," said Rosa, round-eyed at the thought.

CHAPTER V

How it came out at last was like this: Beatriz and his little Nina were talking a day or two later after supper. She and Beatriz and Juliano were sitting on some big cottonwood stumps which they kept in the *placita* for the purpose. On this evening they had rolled them over beside the ditch where they could look up and see the stars, and the lights in other houses in the valley. Diamond, the one-eyed ancient rag of a family dog, was curled at their feet and suddenly he raised his head and let out a gruff half-bark, followed by a series of full-throated angry bellows, having got lamely to his feet.

"That's funny," said Beatriz. "He doesn't often bark like that any more, since he got old and deaf."

"No, except——" Nina looked around in the darkness. "Except the other night he did. Just like that ——" And then she clapped a hand over her mouth, attracting attention to the words which might otherwise have passed unmarked.

The air around them was instantly electric.

Juliano said: "I didn't hear him. What night was that?"

Poor little Nina. Her wits were unequal to a test like this. "Why," she stammered, "I—I guess it was the night you were in town."

Juliano stood up. "Did anybody come here the night we were in town?" he demanded with no effort to conceal his anger.

"I—I don't know, Juliano. I thought I heard——"

Beatriz grasped her wrist then, but it was too late. Juliano turned away and walked into the house where Rosa could be heard humming a tune.

Nina and Beatriz listened intently. The humming stopped. Their hearts were in their throats.

"What was it, little Nina? Anything?"

"Oh, Mary, Mother of God," Nina wailed. "What have I done?"

Beatriz held her wrist more tightly, squeezed it. "What was it, little Nina? Tell me."

She began to cry. "It was Ben Ortiz—I saw him in the moonlight. I got up and looked out when the dog barked. I—I was a little scared. Oh, I wasn't going to tell!"

Beatriz patted her gently. "Never mind, Nina—listen."

No sound from the house—yet. Then they could hear Juliano's voice, in a rising key, and Rosa's, shrill, shrill, denying. Then silence again, for a long time. Nina clung to her husband's big hand with both her slender ones.

Rosa saw, the minute Juliano entered the doorway, that something was wrong. No mistaking that look on his face. She had coped with it so many times before, though, that she had no fear this time. She went on about her business, but her humming stopped—that was the only sign she gave that she knew his intent. And Juliano stood by the door staring at her, trying to wear her down by the force of his concentration.

He might have known better. He had to surrender at last and sit down in a chair, a stiff, straight-backed chair that made him sit up like a schoolboy. Rosa was humming again.

"Rosa."

She stopped in the middle of the room with a kettle in her hand, and waited without answering him.

His eyes fell away from the inquiry in her open gaze. It was hard to look Rosa in the eye, except when love lay in them. Then it was the easiest thing in the world.

"Well?"

Juliano's face twitched with the tumult of things he might choose to say to her. What he wanted to say most he could not. It wouldn't fit into his design. "Rosa, Rosa, I die for love of you!" That was what he wanted to cry out to her. But how could he? Then, as he stared, he felt absurd, hot tears just behind his eyes, ready to spill out and make a fool of him. So he spoke quickly before they could come and dissolve him in their flow. "Rosa!" He heard his voice. It was a plea, not an accusation. But he came to accuse her! He tried again. "Rosa!" There, that was a little better.

By this time Rosa had lowered the kettle to the end of her arm. She made a mocking face at him and tapped her toe impatiently on the dirt floor. "Well, what do you want? How long do I have to stand here?"

"Rosa——" he tried fixing her again with his eyes. "When was Ben Ortiz here?"

Wasn't that a flicker of alarm that crossed her face? Wasn't it a shadow of fear? He pressed what he thought was his advantage. "That night I was in town, Rosa—was Ben here that night?"

Rosa looked away. "Of course not. Nina and I were alone. Oh, he may have been here—but I didn't see him. Did you ask Nina?"

"Yes."

"What did she say?"

Just a suspicion of anxiety in her voice?

Calmly, Juliano said: "Nina says that somebody came here that night—the dog barked—but she didn't know who it was."

Rosa seemed imperceptibly relieved. "Well, why should I know who it was? We were both in bed."

"Rosa, you're lying. I can see it in your eyes."

She turned on him and hesitated. For the first time

she saw that old methods would not do. For a minute
she was baffled. The accusation was there now, all
right, gleaming in his eyes. She had never seen it so
strong; it had never held her tranced like this before.
What was happening to her? She put the kettle on
the stove and sat down on the bed, gaining time. It
was as if Juliano knew the truth already. Did he
know? She stole a quick glance at his face. It gave
her no reassurance. Was her invulnerability desert-
ing her at last? She began to be really frightened
and, struggling not to show it in her face, turned
away from him again. And quickly she faced him
then, full of pretended anger to hide her fear.

"I'm *not* lying! You don't know anything about it.
You weren't even here."

Juliano for once was not deceived. Seeing the rising
panic in her he waited, staring his accusation. He
waited a long time and then he said: "Rosa, did you
never love me?"

"Yes," she threw at him with a toss of her head.

"And do you—still?"

"Yes."

"Why do you always lie?"

Rosa gaped her surprise. "Lie? What makes you
say that?"

"I don't think you love me, Rosa."

She shrugged her ironical shoulders, and Juliano
felt the old pang of thwarted devotion stabbing at his

63

heart; and he knew that he had lost the advantage he had held for a moment. He was pleading again. Something about Rosa made a man her slave. He would rather crawl up to her like a dog and lick her hand than do what he meant to do, what he had to do this time. He sat looking at her intensely for another long interval, while Rosa preened her glossy hair with her finger-tips. She was confident again, he could see that. It was all right. It would be easier to take her by surprise again, when she was not on her guard, not wary and full of guile.

"You are vain, Rosa," he said at last.

"Vain? Am I?"

"Yes. You love yourself too much. Once you loved me, though. I know that. What changed you, Rosa?"

"I never said I had changed. You said that. You seem to know all about it—all about me."

"Yes. I know all about you. I've lost you for some reason, Rosa. Lost you."

She was touched by the pain in his voice and for a moment regretted everything and hated herself. But not for long. He was just being sorrowful, sorry for himself. But she tried to say a gentle thing, and the words fell hollowly on her own ears. "No, you haven't lost me, Juliano. I'm your wife. I——"

Mother of God, she couldn't say it! Now the panic had her tightly. She couldn't say she loved him. Oh, this was terrible!

"Do you think," Juliano was saying in a mono-tonous voice which was beginning to sound like doom in her ears, "do you think you could love me and Ben Ortiz, too?"

She didn't answer, not trusting herself.

"Ben Ortiz has a way with him, hasn't he?" the voice seemed to come now not from Juliano, but from some far place beyond the horizon. "Ben Ortiz is a nice man, isn't he, Rosa? Nice to the girls? He knows how to give a girl a good time. He knows how to love. You don't have to have him around all the time. You don't have to feed him, and sleep in his bed every night, listen to him snore. He comes alone in the night, in the moonlight, in the sunlight, and he gives you a kiss and goes away again. He makes you feel good, doesn't he? He makes you feel beauti-ful and free and happy like an angel."

Rosa glanced at her husband. He was sitting there stiffly in his chair, talking through a kind of tormented smile and his eyes were slits looking at her. She shuddered.

"Stop it, Juliano! Why do you talk like this?"

"You like to have Ben Ortiz come to you like that, don't you, Rosa? You don't love Ben Ortiz, but you love his kisses and his arms. You don't love him as much as you love me. You don't love him as much as you love yourself." Suddenly Juliano's voice rose to a thunder. "You don't love anybody as much as you love yourself, Rosa! You have an evil eye! You're bad! Bad, bad, bad!"

"Stop talking like that!" Rosa screamed. "You're crazy, Juliano. I don't know what you're talking about. Go away from here! You're mad!"

"No, I'm not mad," his voice was even and low again. "I'm not mad. But it was Ben Ortiz, wasn't it? *Wasn't it?*"

Juliano stood up, and in two great strides was beside her, cringing on the bed.

Rosa blanched. Her voice caught in her throat like a death rattle.

"It was Ben Ortiz who was here the night I was in town. Tell me it was! Tell me it was, and I'll teach him to come sneaking into my house when I'm not here. Tell me!"

Rosa broke. She flung herself on the bed whimpering. "Yes, it was Ben Ortiz. He came to me. He was nice to me." She raised her tear-smeared face to Juliano and screamed at him: "I'm glad he came! I hope he comes again, if you want to know——"

Then Juliano struck her. He knocked her off the bed on to the floor, where she lay inert. He stooped over her, turned her face up and struck her twice with his open hand, once on each side of the face, hard. Then he went out.

Beatriz and Nina, transfixed a few feet from the door, heard the blows and trembled. Nina clung to

66

Beatriz as if she herself were being beaten, and buried her face in the crook of his arm, while Beatriz stared and stared at the light from the window. When Juliano appeared at the door, Beatriz gently disentangled himself from Nina and went after him, vanishing in the shadows under the trees. Nina started after them, wringing her hands, stopped, hesitated, and ran into the house where Rosa was.

"Juliano! Stop! Wait! Where are you going? What are you going to do?"

Beatriz caught up with his brother and seized him by the arm. Juliano shook him off like a dog. "Leave me alone," he growled. "This is my business."

"Please, Juliano, wait—think what you're doing."

Juliano stopped and spoke deliberately to him. "Beatriz, go back to the house. You can't do anything with me. I don't want you to come. Now go back."

They were standing in the lane, leading to the valley road. Beatriz heard and stood a moment full of indecision. He was no coward, but the inevitableness in Juliano's voice made him obey. He turned and walked into the shadows of the trees in the *placita*. From there he could watch Juliano marching down the lane in the cloud-scattered moonlight. Presently he followed, short-cutting across a field. No, he wouldn't try to intercept him again, but he'd keep an eye on him.

67

And Juliano advanced darkly along the road, up the valley towards the house of Ben Ortiz. His eyes saw nothing on either side and only the thread of moon-greyed road ahead; and all that he saw was ringed about by red licking flames, as if he looked through a hole in a sheet of fire. The road rose and fell before him, he stepped out airily, seeming not to touch the ground at all, but he progressed, and came at length to Ben's gate. It was shut. He fumbled at the wire which held it, loosed it, flung the gate wide and left it open, a thing a man would never do ordinarily. And he marched up the lane which mounted to the low rise where Ben's house stood. Pausing a moment before the door, Juliano decided not to knock; instead he opened it with a crash and stepped across the threshold.

Ben was still sitting at the supper table in the circle of yellow light cast by an oil-lamp in the centre of it, and his wife and oldest son were there also. He couldn't see Juliano's face because of the glare, but the brash entrance of the man warned him of trouble.

"Who is it? What do you want?" Then he saw him, standing above the lamp. "Oh—it's you."

"Come outside. Ben Ortiz. I want to talk to you."

Ben's wife began to wail, and his son to cry. Trouble, as yet unspoken, was thick in the air.

Ben, on guard, passed outside with Juliano and

shut the door after him. "What do you want of me, Juliano?"

At the sight of the man, Juliano could scarcely control his voice, but he choked through his anger: "You came to my house and took my wife while I was gone, Ben Ortiz. For that I am going to——"

"Wait a minute, Juliano——" Ben spoke with assurance. "Your wife is nothing to me. But when a woman comes whoring after a man, the best thing he can do is give her what she wants——"

Ben got no further. Juliano was on him like a wild-cat, hissing and lashing out, and they rolled on the ground. Ready as he was for anything, Ben had been taken off guard by Juliano's lightning spring, and he went down—underneath.

It was over quickly. Juliano got to his feet—the blade of a knife glittered in his hand, catching the light from the door, thrown open by Ben's screaming wife when she heard the scuffle. And Ben was lying on the ground, groaning.

Juliano turned about and walked slowly down the lane to the valley road, oblivious to the screams of the woman which would rouse the entire valley.

Out of the darkness from nowhere Beatriz appeared and walked beside his brother.

"What did you do, Juliano? Are you all right?"

"Yes, I'm all right. Where did you come from, Beatriz? You followed me after all."

"Yes. Did you kill him?"

"No. I didn't kill him."

"Why not?"

"Because—I don't know." Juliano couldn't tell the truth. He had meant to kill him, when he went there. But those words—oh, how they rang ironical in his ears still, how they seared to his heart and singed his soul! Your wife is nothing to me—but when a woman comes whoring after a man. . . .

He knew they were true. Oh, Rosa, Rosa! No one must ever know. Not even Beatriz—good, kind Beatriz, following like a faithful dog.

Juliano walked in silence. Beatriz couldn't see the big tears which poured from his eyes, nor know the bitter sorrow in his heart. No anger was left in Juliano now—only anguish and destruction. Oh, Rosa, Rosa! That a woman could bring a man to this—make a murderer of him and cast his immortal soul to hell!

Juliano walked in silence, Beatriz following a pace behind, wondering.

Nothing of the airy spring was in Juliano's steps now as they walked slowly back to the Trujillo house. He trudged like a tired animal, stumbling now and again, and hanging his head low. Sometimes Beatriz thought he would fall, and stepped forward to help him. The brother looked back over his shoulder frequently, for he could hear sounds coming from the house of Ben Ortiz, shouts and cries and a growing commotion. The wife must have spread the news and the alarm—but Juliano, never once looking back, never even raising his head to see where he was going, walked in silence.

Beatriz was worried. Once a man carrying a lantern passed them running and stopped when he had gone by so fast that they didn't recognize each other, and said: "Have you heard the news? Ben Ortiz has been knifed by a man—he may die." And dashed on.

Even this failed to rouse Juliano from his silent, stumbling progress, while Beatriz marvelled that news could travel so fast. He must hide Juliano to-night—they might come after him, enraged by the bloody deed. To-morrow would be time enough for explanations. He advanced and shook Juliano by the shoulders.

"Hurry, Juliano. You mustn't sleep in the house to-night. They may come after you. Did you hear that man?"

"Sleep?" said Juliano dreamily. "Did you say sleep, Beatriz?" He laughed hollowly. "How is Rosa, Beatriz? Did I hurt her? How is my little Rosa?"

Beatriz took his brother strongly by the arm and forced him along at a faster pace. It was just like handling a drunken man.

"Come along, Juliano. We've got to hurry."

Beatriz and Cruz, who was back from an evening of singing when they returned, fixed a bed in a shed for Juliano and laid him there, tractable as a babe. Then they went into the house and discussed the whole affair in whispers, with Nina sitting tensely by.

Rosa was still hysterical, in her own room. They sat in the kitchen, the two men on the bed, Nina rigidly upright in a chair.

"How is Rosa, Nina?"

"She's better now. She cried all the time you were gone. I couldn't do anything with her."

"Did she say anything?"

"No, not much. She just cried and cried."

And suddenly, while they talked softly, Rosa herself came in. Nobody spoke. Her eyes were red-rimmed and moist and her dark skin was mottled from the bruises, where Juliano had struck her. They looked at her hard at first, full of their anger at her shame, but the sight of her, beaten and distraught, was too much for Beatriz. His kind heart melted and he rose and went to her.

"How are you, Rosa?"

"I'm all right," she said thickly, her voice still laden with sobs. "Where's Juliano?"

"We fixed him up a bed in the shed, out in the corral. He's all right."

"What did he do? Did he—go to—Ben?"

"Yes."

"Did he—kill him?" Rosa sank into a chair.

"No."

"Oh, it's all my fault," and her whole body shook again with sobbing.

Beatriz motioned them all outside, leaving Rosa alone.

"I think I'd better go back and see how Ben is," he said. "You stay here, Cruz, and you, Nina, go to bed. I'll be back soon."

Beatriz met three groups of men on the valley road, returning to their homes, and he stopped to talk to all of them. He was relieved to find no anger in them. It was a simple case of revenge, they thought. What must be, must be. Certainly it was none of their affair. It was too bad—they were only afraid that this was not the end of it. That Ben Ortiz was a crazy man when he was angry. They hoped he would let it pass. No, he was not badly hurt—a wound in his shoulder, a flesh cut in his arm.

Beatriz walked on.

"I'm sorry this happened," he said to Ben's wife when he reached her house which was deserted of visitors now.

"Do you want to see him?" she said.

"If he wants to see me."

She showed him to another room where Ben lay on a bed, smoking a cigarette.

"Hello, Ben. I'm sorry my brother did this to you. I hope you're not hurt badly."

"No. Not bad. Tell your brother Juliano to look

73

out for me—and to keep that wife of his chained up."
Thereupon Ben closed his eyes and refused to say
more.

Little remained to be said, but as Beatriz was leaving, Ben's wife walked outside with him. "I guess he
had it coming to him," she said as Beatriz walked
away.

CHAPTER VI

Rosa was not all contrition. Her surrender to Juliano's will and fury was abject for a while. She whimpered like a beaten dog, and cowered and cringed and begged forgiveness with soft, beseeching eyes.

But this mood passed when she saw that Ben Ortiz had not been killed and that Juliano was much as he had always been, after the storm. Rebellion flared again in her heart. Why should she be treated like a cow? Or a fractious mare, beaten into submission? Why should she?

She began to sulk. And she was delighted to see that she still had power over him. She caught him watching her on the sly, studying her face and her mood, trying to discover what they concealed. He was sorry he had beaten her, then. Ah, she'd make him pay dearly for that. What sorrow and remorse those blows would cost him!

She continued to sulk. And she never addressed a word to him unless he asked it, and then she spoke shortly, with what amounted to a snarl. He always caved in under such treatment, always had in the past, and she thought he would this time. And as the days passed she was sure of it. He was beginning to weaken. He watched her more and more, and many times she could tell that he was on the point of speaking to her about it, and lost his courage before the words came.

She dangled him at the end of her disfavour and made him leap and dance like a toy, until Juliano, in his turn, became abject in his surrender. It took more courage to assault her silence than to march up to Ben Ortiz with a knife in his hand. She was far more dangerous. Her weapons could hurt and slay and reduce a man to a living death. Power, it was; evil, supernatural force with smiling eyes.

Juliano wilted under it. He began to see the cold, chiselled mask of her face even in his dreams, and it always wore a smile which was its cutting edge. He tried to lose himself in work. He finished the well. Having belched black smoke and shuddered in its bowels, it yielded water at last. Juliano was proud and asked Rosa to come and see what he had done.

She turned her back on him. "What of it? You've been at it long enough," she said.

Juliano flinched and went out alone to stand beside his well, looking down into its black depths as if he wished he were hiding there.

It was not enough, not nearly enough, after a week of it. He was only beginning to suffer. Rosa gauged

the effect of her revenge accurately and skilfully. She
well knew the signs. He had begun to hang his head
in her presence, a plea had entered into his voice
again, whenever he spoke to her. And at last the
moment came she had been waiting for.

"Rosa," he cried one night when the others had
gone to bed. "Why do you treat me like this? Why
won't you speak to me any more?"

Oh, at last! She turned slowly to him. Already her
breath was heaving and her eyes went wide and narrow by turns as her fury mounted. Her teeth came
together, her parted lips revealed them clenched
evenly along the front, and her jaw set in a hard,
fixed line.

Before she said a word, Juliano was sorry he had
spoken.

"Speak to you," she hissed. "After what you did to
me? Speak to you! I'm never going to speak to you
again. Never! I'm going to make you sorry for what
you've done to me. I can do it. I can't beat you but
I can make you crawl and lick my hand——" She
drew out these last words and made them sound
hideous.

"But, Rosa, I——"

"You have nothing to say to me!" She raised her
voice and stopped him by drowning his words in her
own. "You're going to pay for what you've done to
me, Juliano. Some day you're going to come to me

and beg me to forgive you, and I won't forgive you. I'll spit in your face like this——"

She spat at him and he turned his head away in a quick, inadvertent motion. And her voice had a tragic tremor as she went on: "Oh, you don't know what you did to me that night! I didn't hurt you. I didn't hurt anybody by what I did. If you had never known about it, what difference would it have made? Just because you found out, because you're mean and jealous and bad and cruel, you beat me and killed something in me that I felt for you and made a fool of yourself with Ben Ortiz. Yes, you're the one who made a fool of himself, not me! I didn't do anything wrong. If I wanted Ben Ortiz to be nice to me I asked him to. I don't have to tell you about it. I won't tell you about it, ever. I'll do as I please from now on, and if you beat me again I'll kill you. I'll tell Ben Ortiz and he'll kill you!"

All the time she watched Juliano's face and noted what effect her words were having there. When she saw now that the present trend was not right, that Juliano was threatening to rise out of his submission at this talk of Ben Ortiz, she changed her tune. And her voice was more tragic than ever when she said: "I'm only a girl. I didn't know anything. You could have been kind instead of beating me in the face and kicking me around on the floor."

"I didn't kick——"

LITTLE VALLEY

"Oh, don't think I don't know what you did. I was
there, wasn't I? It was me you were beating, not
another man. A woman, a girl, your wife! A fine
man, to do a thing like that! For the rest of your
life you ought to be ashamed. I'll never be the same
again. You hurt me. Not only my face and my arms
and my legs and my shoulders. All of them you hurt,
but you hurt more here!" She beat her breast and
raised her eyes to the ceiling and saw with savage
joy that Juliano's were cast down. "I'll never be the
same again!" she finished with a final lift of her
head.

Juliano sat motionless, his head down, his hands
folded in his lap. At last he raised his eyes to her, and
they were moist. "I'm sorry, Rosa—for what I've
done."

She turned her back on him and ignored his
apology. Juliano went outside and slept in the shed
where he had slept that first night after knifing Ben
Ortiz.

But Rosa was not through with him yet. Deeper
shades of punishment were still in her mind. She
continued to sulk through the days and to drive him
out of her bed at night. That he would never go to
another woman she knew too well. He was a faithful
man, deep down in his nature. He was far too shy
ever to seduce or be seduced, except by Rosa herself.
She had this in mind also. When the right time came

79

she could make him hers again after one night in his bed. So easy it was. But the time was not ripe. He had to suffer more and pay and pay.

When she heard that he was up again, she went to see Ben Ortiz. But she saw Juliano first. She dressed herself in her best clothes and left in front of her blouse a voluptuous glimpse of the parting of her breast. And she went to Juliano with a wanton smile and sway of her hips.

"I'm going up to see Ben Ortiz," she said, "after what you've done to him. I'm going to see if he's all right."

Juliano stared at her. His face was hard and immovable. He turned at last and walked away from her without speaking, and she followed him with a sparkling laugh.

She found Ben in his field, irrigating his wheat. He didn't come to her on the run this time, but left her standing there by the fence unnoticed. When she called to him, he put down his hoe deliberately and walked to her.

"Hello, Rosa. What are you doing here?"

"I came to see how you were, Ben."

He looked at her suspiciously. "Me? Nothing's the matter with me. You mean that little scratch your crazy husband gave me?" He laughed scornfully. "That's nothing."

"I'm sorry he did that, Ben."

"You're sorry, are you? What did you tell him for then?"

"I didn't tell him."

Ben pushed his *sombrero* back on his forehead and leaned heavily on the top wire. "Tell me, Rosa—why did you come to me that day? You don't love me— do you?"

Rosa picked a spear of grass and stuck it between her teeth. She must be sure to say the right thing, now. And with lowered eyes she said: "Oh, I do in a way, Ben. You're really very nice——"

Ben straightened and threw out his chest with a laugh. "Well, that's all right, then." But he grew instantly serious and shook his finger under her nose. "But if I thought you were playing with me, getting me into trouble for nothing, I'd—I'd——"

"You'd what?" She gave him a wide smile.

Ben scratched his head. "Well, I'd do something about it. I might kick you right up the valley road and back into the arms of that fool of a husband of yours."

"Oh, no, Ben——"

"What's the matter? Don't you like him? Isn't he nice to you?"

"Juliano? Oh, yes, I like him all right."

"But you like me better, no? Is that it?"

She nod·'ed shyly.

Leaning far over the fence, Ben said: "Maybe you

F   81

and me could get together again some time, Rosa."

She had begun to edge away. "Maybe," she said and started to walk away. "I'm glad you're better, Ben," she called back.

"Ah, he didn't hurt me. If I'd known he was coming I'd have been ready for him. See you soon, Rosa." And Ben went back to his work with a song on his lips.

And Rosa had a little fear in her heart as she walked home. She didn't know Ben as well as Juliano, wasn't sure of him, could not anticipate him as surely as Juliano. She hoped she hadn't said too much. Love Ben Ortiz? No, no. She hoped he wouldn't come around and make a nuisance of himself like an old stallion. If he did she'd have to send him away for good. The idea wasn't to get Ben all excited again, but to punish Juliano. But Ben didn't know that. She might have to tell him some time. Then he would be mad.

She chuckled and clasped her shoulders in her hands, thinking how mad Ben would be. And she skipped down the road because she was excited, and all this intrigue made her heart gay. She was playing a winning game, she knew that, but it was rather dangerous. And she didn't want any more fighting. Men were such fools. Their brains were all in their fists. When they didn't know what else to do they fought, as if that ever settled anything. Well, at least she had the immense satisfaction of showing Juliano that she wasn't afraid of him. Under his very nose she had gone back to Ben Ortiz and apologized for him. She couldn't think how Juliano's cup could be made more bitter. Perhaps it was time to get him back now. She didn't want to run the risk of losing him. She laughed and laughed as she skipped down the road.

Juliano discovered that he could sulk, too. It didn't seem to bother Rosa much—not nearly as much as her sulking bothered him. But he thought it had a slight effect. It worried her a little. And the war went on, waning little by little until at last it required too much effort to keep it going.

CHAPTER VII

THE black wings of disaster, having shadowed the Trujillo brothers, passed on. Juliano was himself again at last, and the old impudent sway returned to Rosa's hips when she walked. But they didn't speak to each other much, though they lived together in the two rooms and preserved former appearances. Even their silence would pass in time, the others knew. What must be, must be.

The furrows carved in Juliano's face by the night of sorrow remained there, and Rosa was a shade less gay. None of them, in fact, was quite the same afterwards, but people are always being changed by one thing or another. The greatest change was in Juliano —he smiled even more rarely than before.

And he worked harder and played less. Time passed swiftly as the harvest season approached. And Ben Ortiz, if he had thoughts of revenge, gave no sign.

It was the season of storms and swift, dark descents of clouds. The land demanded the attention of men, whose eyes were held skyward. Up and down the valley the second stand of alfalfa was being cut, and the air was heavy with the strong sweet scent. Dogs followed in the wake of scythes, to pounce upon hapless field-mice revealed by the falling grasses.

Juliano thought much about his deed. Now that it was in the past, he could look back upon it with something like calm and judgment. He was glad he hadn't killed Ben Ortiz, but he was not sorry for what he had done.

He thought this way as he swung his scythe in rhythmic great sweeps and the dog—the same deaf dirty woollen lump of a beast who had brought down the black vulture of evil—waddled grossly behind and sniffed disdainfully at field-mice, his pink tongue lolling the while.

It was good to be back on the land! And Rosa— even Rosa seemed not all bad, working hard as she was over her vegetables, true to her promise to provide the family with greens through the winter. And little Nina, helping, always unobtrusively helping.

But she was pregnant again, Rosa said, and one dark thought hovered in the back of Juliano's mind. How did he know it wasn't the child of Ben Ortiz? Could he look upon this new child with love and trust? It was hard for them to mention his name now in a conversation, but he had asked her about it, and she had said it was impossible—it must be Juliano's own child. And how she seemed to have changed, that Rosa! She was all his now. She never wanted to go to the *bailes* on Saturday nights and when the priest was in the valley she wanted to be near him all the time.

Yes, life seemed good again to Juliano. The harvest would be full, the rains fell often enough and none of them came with a roar and a flood, to leave devastation behind, as they did in fiercer seasons. The rain, it seemed sometimes, was bent on robbing them of what little land they had, the way it swelled the stream and roared out of the canyon above the valley and swept over their fields. The stoutest dikes they built were melted like piles of sand.

But none of that this year. The land was repaying him for the blows which fate had dealt his soul through the night of sorrow.

In the narrow life of Vallecito it was inevitable that Juliano and Ben Ortiz should meet occasionally. They were careful not to cross one another, and they got on well enough with few words spoken. But anybody could see that they were enemies. Forgiveness was not in their hearts. When Ben's corn wanted cutting, Beatriz and Cruz were on hand to help, but not Juliano; and Ben stayed away when the Trujillo fields were ready.

Rosa's patch of vegetables kept her busy for a week. She left the cabbages in the ground, and charged the two boys to keep the rabbits away from them, which they did faithfully until the game lost its savour. And the men, when the harvest was done, hauled wood for the winter and made another trip to town to buy a rope for the well, and other necessary things.

Juliano decided at the last moment to go with them. This time he rode a horse and carried two young pigs in the saddlebags to sell in the town. It would probably be their last trip until the spring, so they took all their burros loaded with wood and every possible surplus to raise as much cash as they could.

He left Rosa without fear now; they joined another caravan bound on a similar errand. One man had brought his guitar and they sang when they stopped to rest.

And it was a lucky thing the harvest was good, for soon after they returned from the town, Cruz announced his intention of marrying a certain girl he had met there. The business of courtship over such a distance was complicated and costly as well, not to count the expense of buying the girl's clothes and gifts.

Now was the time, Cruz decided, to agitate for that house he had planned long ago when old Pablo had died. He showed the brothers the place he had selected for it and they shook their heads. It was too late in the year, it would soon be too cold to lay adobes. But Cruz won out because the adobes were all made and lying in rows in the *placita*. He pleaded

with Juliano and pointed out how they might dissolve and be useless by spring if left to stand in the
snows all winter. Having no father or mother, Cruz
turned to his oldest brother for help and guidance,
and Juliano gave it willingly, as best he could. He
tried to look severe and dignified when he called on
the girl's family in the town and made the arrange-
ments for the wedding. They couldn't be married
until well into the winter, because the priest came to
Vallecito only once in three weeks; but that didn't
really matter, said the girl, because they would be
married in the cathedral in the town.

How fast things moved now! And to add to the
complications it came about that Nina would have
her first child in the early spring. They would be
needing that additional house now, all right, and the
sooner the better. So the three brothers spent all their
days working on the house for Cruz, and it rose
steadily. Cruz himself went into the mountains to cut
the beams for the roof, taking both horses and enough
food to stay three days. He camped high up where
the tall pines grew and the stream which watered
their valley was a mountain brook. In the mornings
its edges were fringed with ice, transparent and thin.
He slept on a sheepskin, with bright-coloured native
blankets over him for warmth, and his sleep was
deep, his dreams were fair. Having cut all the trees
he needed in two days, he stayed on because he liked

88

it up there and he wanted to bring back some fish for the others. Something about this high mountain country was restful and satisfying after the red lands below. Perhaps it was the abundance of water, and the green meadows, the great solemn trees growing neatly alone without underbrush, as if some master gardener kept them trim.

Most of all it was the peace he loved. It was far beyond him to comprehend, beyond the power of man to change. The pattern of struggle against the reluctant earth which had made him what he was released him here and something else was permitted to flow in and out of him like a freshening breeze. Freedom, peace, stillness.

When he returned to the valley, Cruz and Beatriz went back as far as they could with a wagon, where Cruz had piled his logs, and brought them in, and when the men finished laying the roof, Nina and Rosa went down to plaster the house, inside and out. With practised hands they threw mud on the walls and smoothed it caressingly with their palms.

There, the house was finished. It seemed no time at all since they dug the first trench and poured in rock and mud for the foundations. To be sure, it was only one small room with a hearth in the corner, but it was a house! His own house, made with his own two hands. What more could a bride require? Cruz, in the intervening days, used to stop his work, whatever it was, and slip down to his house and stand and look at it by the hour.

On a day in the autumn, when the land was never so resplendent in gold and red and the dry leaves crackled on the oak-brush, the whole Trujillo family went in to the town for the *prendorio*, the engagement feast. They made one wagon-load. Juliano drove the team and Rosa sat up on the driver's seat beside him, and the others bounced in the body of the wagon on heaps of homespun blankets. They left very early in the morning in order to arrive on time. Rosa's two boys were pop-eyed and frisky before they pulled out of the valley; and the horses went so slowly up the hills that the boys were on the ground half the time, running along beside the wagon.

Then Juliano would make the team run down the other sides of the hills and the children would be left howling and yelling far behind, and those in the wagon thought it a great joke, in spite of the terrific shaking-up they got from the bumps in the road.

Oh, it was a high-spirited wagon-load who drove from Vallecito to the town that day. They pulled up before the house of Cruz's bride at one o'clock, and that ended their hilarity for the time. It wouldn't do to appear before the new family all dishevelled and full of laughter. One must be solemn and dignified. Rosa took the two boys in hand and had them subdued in no time, transformed from shrieking little devils into round-eyed, dark-skinned cherubim.

They were met at the door by the bride's father, and ushered into the house without a smile. The bride herself was nowhere to be seen. Inside, the mother waited, dressed in sober black silk with old white lace trimmings at the collar and wrists. She looked so grand and rich and beautiful that the Trujillo women were awed by her, and stared.

Rosa, never so meek before, held her eyes cast down and spoke in hardly audible tones, clutching her two boys hard by the hands lest they do some mischief. But she saw everything. She examined the house, the furniture, the pictures, the linen minutely, and within ten minutes had a complete catalogue of all in her mind. All that she could see, at any rate. And she felt better about it. Their things were no better than hers—newer, some of them, but no better. Many were not so good. Newness had not yet come to be a virtue on its own account.

The visitors were given chairs around the walls as at a wake, and to be sure the atmosphere was not dissimilar. No laughter, no gaiety. They sat stiffly on the chairs and stared at the white walls of the room where family photographs, tinted under bulging glass, stared woodenly back at them.

At last other guests began to come and the formality eased. By three o'clock the house was full of people. Cruz brought in the trunk of gifts for the bride and set it down inside the door, the bride appeared to receive it, and after very formal introductions all around the party was on. Three players came in, two guitars and a banjo, and played spritely tunes and people started to talk naturally. Rosa's spirits lifted.

Soon she was moving about among the guests with ease and her hips were swaying as of old and her eyes were getting in their work. These men of the town were shy at first, but she soon broke through their reserve.

As Rosa's gaiety increased, Juliano's diminished. He kept an eye on her, and many old misgivings were reborn. She was the same Rosa, then. He saddened. The same Rosa. Wanton, flirtatious, wicked. If only he didn't love her so! Look, how she captured that boy in the blue serge suit—how he followed her about like a dog, his tongue hanging out. If he could only be gay like that himself, but beside Rosa in this mood he felt heavy and lifeless. He took a drink of whisky from a table spread with delicacies and wine for the ladies, hard drink for the men. Ah, that was better. Two or three more and he'd be able to forget Rosa.

That was the thing to do, forget her and have some fun with the girls himself. But he couldn't do it without drink. And sometimes even that failed.

It failed him now. Juliano drank up to the limit he dared, and the more he swallowed the more morose he became. So he left the house altogether and wandered alone through the streets of the town.

And all through the evening at the dance which followed the feast he talked soberly with the bride's father about crops and farms and politics and the future of Cruz Trujillo. Out of the corner of his eye he caught glimpses of Rosa, always with a different man, always rolling her eyes at him and twisting her hips like a wanton.

They went home in the morning. And Juliano could find little in his heart to rejoice him. Rosa sat beside him as before, and they hardly spoke. As the female representative of the family, she had been a doubtful benefit, he felt, for he had seen the bride's father eyeing her without approval more than once. So he held his tongue, full of such thoughts as these, but unwilling to speak them out because Rosa had had such a good time.

Only one thing remained before the wedding, and that was the *fiesta* in the valley for the bride's family. They had agreed to make the trip on the same day in the following week—Cruz was so anxious for the girl to see the place.

Everybody in the valley came to meet the bride of Cruz Trujillo. Apart, they debated whether to invite

Ben Ortiz or not, and in the end they decided they would. And Ben, to everybody's surprise, came and acted as if nothing were wrong with the thing. He got a little drunk on some strong, home-made wine and paid boisterous attention to the girls, but avoiding Rosa, carefully avoiding Rosa.

It was a warm day, and they were gathered in the *placita* under the cottonwoods, a noisy crowd of people, Ben with his fiddle singing and dancing about, Juliano in their midst, sober but not unhappy. Ben was standing on top of a table playing his fiddle and stamping in time with his foot.

Suddenly he stopped and pointed with the bow towards Rosa's cabbage patch. "Look," he cried, "a rabbit is eating the cabbages!"

Everybody turned about to see, some started throwing stones. And Juliano stopped them, rushing into the thick of the crowd.

"Wait!" he called in a great voice. "Wait—I'll get him." And he dashed into the house, reappearing in a moment with the old rifle his father had left to him. Walking to the edge of the crowd he pointed the gun at the rabbit and all eyes followed his aim.

The explosion nearly knocked him down and simultaneously came a splash in the cabbage patch where the rabbit had been.

An applauding shout went up. Juliano lowered his gun slowly, looked at it tenderly, patted its gleaming barrel. And as he walked by Ben Ortiz to return the gun to its place above his bed, he gave his enemy a look which chilled the hearts of those who saw it.

It was some time before the *fiesta* recovered its former spirit.

PART TWO

CHAPTER I

JULIANO had not long to worry about his Rosa. Time took care of that. She remained always a woman with ready laughter and a wandering eye, but fifteen years took her physical beauty—the wonder was that she kept it as long as she did. Now, with a white towel wrapped around her once gleaming, blue-black hair and six children, one grown up, in her house, it wanted an effort of remembering to recall the lithe, wanton creature she once had been.

Things had changed in the valley, too. It had grown more populous, among other things. Cruz had a family, Beatriz had a family; up and down the valley the people were increasing and no man could guess what would become of all the children. It didn't seem that the narrow fields could take care of them. For even if more land could be cleared and brought under the ditch, the supply of water remained the same—no man could increase that. Long ago they had apportioned the use of the ditch among the farms, and chosen a *mayordomo* to administer it. They had to come to this because people used to have such ferocious fights over water.

It was only occasionally that worries like these came to harass the older men, but when they did they occupied long sunny Sunday hours beside a warm south-facing adobe wall. When they tried to talk it out, they found that nobody could see very far beyond to-morrow, nor beyond the last turning of the stream. God's will be done.

Juliano was bewildered sometimes at the speed with which the world seemed to move nowadays. When he went into the town, that sleepy, dusty place of turning wagon-wheels, what changes struck him speechless! In place of the rutted old streets were brick-paved thoroughfares. Electric lights and automobiles had driven out the soft light of lamps and the lazy wagons. There were none of those devilish engines in Vallecito yet, thank God.

But a man from the country could still sell his wood there, and get a better price for it, too. They could have their noisy newness. A *paisano* could take his money and go home where life was still a quiet flowing.

For the most part, it was peaceful, anyway. Beatriz lost a baby girl, and that was a sad thing. It was his last. Nina was through with breeding after that, discouraged, it seemed, and finished. Rosa was through, too, though Juliano suspected that she could have more if she wanted them. With Nina's four and Rosa's six and Cruz down there with his six more, the Trujillo family could be said to have prospered, if that were prospering. It called for some stretching to feed them all from the original acres, but they did well enough while the water flowed. Each farm could have the use of the ditch only one day a week now.

Let the water fail—ah, nobody liked to think of that.

Ben Ortiz, whose farm lay at the head of the valley where it first widened after the stream left its canyon, claimed that the water was failing. Less and less every year. But Ben was that way. He always believed the worst, now. Something had made him bitter. Nobody knew just what it was. They guessed one thing and another, and agreed pretty generally that it was disappointment over his family, who hadn't turned out as well as a man might hope. He had only three children to begin with, two girls and a boy, and the boy had a withered arm.

So he had no son to send to the war.

Yes, even that strange, far fury was brought to the valley by men in uniform, and they shook their heads over the Ortiz boy's withered arm. And Ben marched him off with his eyes crying defiance. He was just as good as any other lad—he could work a plough and drive a team, cut wood, build a house. If they didn't want him, so much the better. He wouldn't be left alone to do all the work himself. Why should he send off a boy to be killed, anyway? In Vallecito they hardly knew there was a war until the men came to take their boys away.

Juliano's oldest son was taken, and half a dozen others. No flags and stirring music saw them off; like sheep going to market, their wan, frightened faces peering out behind at the only spot of earth they had ever known, they were herded into a vast grey truck which roared out of the valley like a summer storm, its thunder echoing from the hills. And that was all.

The people didn't know what to think about it. That they might be killed was a dim possibility, but incredible. Who would want to kill young, innocent boys like those? No, they'd all come back, and brighten many an hour with tales of adventure and strange lands. Juliano and Rosa settled down to wait for José's return. Not knowing what lay ahead of the boy, they seldom worried about him, only accepted it as people had to accept everything in a tyrant land. Rosa wondered about him now and then, more often than Juliano did.

"Do you think José is all right?" she would say. "We haven't heard from him for a long time."

"Yes, he's all right. They make him write in English—that's why he doesn't write to us—don't you remember, he said so himself."

"Maybe they'll make him learn English."

"Sure. When he comes back we won't know him."

Oh, prophetic innocence!

"I hope he shoots some Germans," Juliano always added boastfully, like a child, wondering in the same breath what Germans were and how they differed from other people, what made them so wicked that the whole world wanted to shoot at them.

But he believed that they must be bad people. Why else would they take a boy out of Vallecito and send him thousands of miles away? Why else would they come into the forgotten little valley and try to make the people buy beautiful scraps of paper called Liberty Bonds?

They had to laugh at that. If a man had a hundred dollars he'd spend it. He'd give some of it to the Church, to rest the souls of the dead, and what was left he'd use for himself. And his family. Nobody was fool enough to buy one of the things, not even the other Trujillo family who had started a store and now had a post-office in it.

Cruz was afraid he might have to go to the war. He stayed away from the town altogether, hoping they wouldn't come again to the valley and ask him more questions. They almost took him the first time. But they didn't come again, and the first thing they knew the war was over. It seemed like no time at all, looking back. They rang the church bells and had a big dance in the new bare hall, from which Ben Ortiz stayed away.

And when the boys came home—all but one—they

had another dance which was an even bigger celebration, and Ben Ortiz did not stay away. He wanted to have a look at these boys who had been to a war and see if it made any difference in them. As for the boy who had not returned, that was too bad. No, he hadn't been killed on the field of battle. He had died ingloriously in a hospital of Spanish influenza. Ah, that was too bad. A boy might at least get a bullet for all his trouble.

And José, he was like a stranger in the house. Juliano sat and stared at him, trying to piece together the fragments of memory with this person who had come back to them. Nothing seemed to fit. The boy made him feel like a stranger, with his talk of aeroplanes and Paris, and all in English, fluent English which nobody could understand.

"Well, José, what are you going to do now?" Juliano said to him. "Glad to be home, no? Lots of work to be done here. Maybe you get married now, no? And start a family?"

José looked coolly at his father, but with an aloof kindness which Juliano couldn't understand. "Maybe," was all he said.

No amount of strangeness could chill the warmth Juliano felt at seeing his son again. He went to the dance with him and made the happy discovery that by drinking with José he could recapture the old feeling of belonging to him.

He got pretty drunk that night. So did most of the men and especially those whose sons came back from the war. As the drink mounted to his head, Juliano's pride increased. Think of having a son who had been taken across the ocean to shoot at Germans!

"How many Germans did you shoot, José? Six? Eight? A hundred?"

"Oho, my son, José—he shot a hundred Germans, he shot. . . ."

He reeled about, in and out of the *baile* hall, shouting his inane story. Nobody paid much attention to him; when he gripped them by their coat-lapels they smiled and broke away from him as soon as they could.

Inside, where the dance was beginning, Rosa sat in a chair along the wall with Nina and Cruz's wife. And the wife of Ben Ortiz was sitting beside Rosa. She was a round lump of a woman, swathed in black as if in mourning for the flock of children she did not have. She spoke to no one, only sat motionless, with her dark eyes darting. And Rosa's face was composed also, but in a different way; always a trace of a smile on Rosa's face, an inward smile as if she knew a huge joke that nobody else knew. Juliano noticed it but never until this night had he mentioned it. Now with the liquor in his head he could say anything that came to mind without weighing it, and he went up to Rosa's chair and stood there in front of her, swaying back and forth on his legs like a tree in the wind. For a long time he only looked at her while his lips twitched and his eyes blinked, and a wary person could almost read the muddle of thoughts which produced these things. And Rosa pretended to be amused meanwhile, talking behind her hand to Nina and giggling, but her heart was skipping, for she knew what might be coming, and hoped Juliano would hold his tongue. Now he was narrowing his eyes at her and stroking his chin with his fingers, and this went on and on, and Rosa began to be nervous. Why didn't he speak, the fool? Why didn't he speak?

"Go away, Juliano," she whispered. "People are laughing at you. Can't you see?"

"Let them laugh," he muttered. "Once you made them laugh at me, you—you witch, you. That's what you are. That's why you're always smiling that way. Now I've found you out." He was raising his voice and pointing a shaking finger at Rosa. For once the smile left her face. "You've got the evil eye, you have! You witch! Witch, witch, *witch!*"

Then he reeled away crying it to all the dancers and all the women seated along the wall like a jury. "She's a witch, she's a witch, she's a witch!"

Rosa shuddered. It was no idle thing to be called a witch, even by a drunken man. Witches were very real in the valley, and greatly feared. And hated. Rosa tried to smile again, but it was a crooked smile.

She looked at the dumpy little wife of Ben Ortiz and saw her immovable, like a figure of stone. Juliano had gone outside, but Rosa still felt uncomfortable, felt many eyes upon her still, hotly. The idiot! The fool! How she hated him! How she had hated him all these years, bearing his children in hate, lying in his bed with hate, taking his hateful seed! When she felt calm again, when the people had forgotten the scene, she left the *baile* and went home.

For it was not the first time she had been called a witch. Her flashing eyes and competent hands had earned her some renown in the valley—not all good. She seemed to have a power in her hands. And while it was working for the good of a neighbour or a friend, it was praised, but let it seem to fail. . . .

Through the years Rosa had made no friends. She was too quick, too brusque to make people like her, though they respected her and even feared her a little. Her tongue could lash out and wound a man or a woman, and her eyes could drill into a person's head and expose the thoughts that were hidden there. Uncanny, some called it. Evil and dangerous, they said.

But she would lend a hand in every extremity and help one and all with strange impartiality. She was the best midwife in the valley. She was the quickest weaver, the deftest with her needle. But she was nowhere loved.

107

It was a strange thing. When she was younger, men had loved her. Ben Ortiz was not the only one. But they all got over it sooner or later, and a few ended by hating her because they said she had an evil eye, and captured them for her pleasure merely, like a cat. Sometimes Rosa thought about it.

She thought about it now as she left the *baile*. She felt, at rare intervals, unbearably lonely. So she felt now, lonely and friendless, joyless, bereft. She would willingly die. Did the people really think she was a witch? What, then, was a witch? A woman who helped wherever she could, brought babies into the world and soothed the suffering? If she found all people wanting in something necessary to her, was that what made her a witch? Was it her fault? Perhaps it was. Other people had friends and were loved. Why, why did she always come away with a feeling of emptiness? Somewhere on the earth was a person she could love, surely. Not one of her own flesh and blood, like José whom she adored, but someone quite outside herself who would be worthy, who would consume her in his fire. That she had never found him was no fault of hers. It was hardly remarkable that she should never find him in a place as small as Vallecito. Why, the people in this place could be counted in a minute and she never had a chance to get out of it.

As for the women, they were only little men, less

than men. If they could flatter a man, refresh him, cause him by their ministrations to his vanity to fling out his chest and clap his wings, they were satisfied. Their work was done. She could not—could not— stoop to that. She didn't know why. Something in her forbade it, that was all. Her life, her mission, contained more. When she saw a man sinking himself into her tenderness like a cool spring, so he could rise refreshed and shout, "Ah, what a man am I!" she revolted and spurned him thenceforth. And that was what they all did—or tried to do. Juliano like the rest.

That was why she held herself aloof, because she felt these things in her heart and could not speak them, for she didn't know what they were. Why should she? She was only a *paisana*, no different, really, from the others. God had given her quick, deft hands and a seeing eye, and it was a curse, where it should have been a boon.

It was cold. Snow lay on the northward slopes of the hills and it gleamed weirdly in the starlight. The ground underfoot was hard like stone. Rosa's footsteps echoed as she put her feet down angrily. Footsteps behind her. She looked back. A man was following her. It wasn't Juliano, for he walked steadily.

"Wait," he said. "It's me—Ben Ortiz."

"Oh. What do you want with me, Ben Ortiz?"

"I—just want to talk to you. Are you going home?"

"Yes, but you can't come there. Are you crazy?"

He was even with her now. "I heard what he said to you." Ben laughed emptily. "The fool. Come. I'll walk home with you."

"Be careful, Ben. Don't make any more trouble. It's been a long time. . . ."

"Yes—a long time. I'm not afraid of him. You're too good for him, anyhow."

"No, I'm not."

"Yes, you are. You should have married me, Rosa. I should have married you instead of that—that dry cow."

"No, Ben. Don't talk like that."

"Why not? It's the truth."

"No."

"Why did he call you a witch?"

"I don't know. He was drunk."

"Drunk?"

"Of course he's drunk. Didn't you see him?"

"But even if he is drunk, that's no reason——"

"I'm not a witch," Rosa said simply. "I don't know what a witch is."

"I don't think you're a witch, Rosa."

They walked a while in silence as far as the Trujillo house and beyond.

"Do you like me, Ben?"

"Yes, of course I like you, Rosa. I—I didn't like you for a long time. I hated you."

"Why?"

"Because I thought you got me into trouble. I thought you were using me to make Juliano jealous. I hated you then. But even when I hated you, I couldn't forget you."

"Do you still hate me?"

"No." He laughed a little. "I got over that all right."

"I'm glad you did, Ben. Because not very many people like me in Vallecito. Why is that, do you suppose?"

"Maybe it's because you don't like many people."

She stopped talking while she thought about this. It was a simple answer to her question, all right.

"We're getting old, Rosa, and—and I guess we don't need to fight as much as we did. I think you and I ought to be real friends again."

Rosa sighed. "I'm very lonely. I wish I could have a real friend again."

"Why don't you come up to my house, Rosa? We're almost there now. We could have a glass of wine——"

Rosa hesitated. Why not? Why not have a glass of wine with Ben Ortiz? He still hates me, really, underneath, she was thinking. You never get over hating—

sometimes you mix it up with love, the way he's doing now, but it's hate.

"All right, Ben. I don't see any harm in that. They'll be at the *baile* for a long time yet."

"Good."

They walked up Ben's road and crossed the ditch on a wooden bridge and entered the *placita* of Ben's house. A cold wind was blowing up there; the house was cold, too, and Ben hurried to get the stove going. In a moment it was hot, with the smelly closeness of an overheated stove. Rosa sat close to it to warm her hands and feet, and Ben joined her there.

"It's been a long time since you were in my house, Rosa."

"Yes, Ben—a long time."

Soon he was up again lighting lamps and pouring two glasses of red wine. Rosa took off her shawl and moved to a more comfortable chair. The wine tasted good and she could feel its tingling warmth all the way down her throat and in her stomach. "Ah," she said.

"Good, isn't it? I get this wine from some friends of mine who have grapes. They live down south on the Rio Grande where it's warm."

"That's a good place to live, I should think. This place is too cold for grapes—or anything else."

"No, I have a grape vine. It does pretty good——"

And then a difficulty, a shyness, came over them

and, widening, became an enemy to talk. They assaulted the enemy half-heartedly for a while. At last Ben moved his chair close to Rosa for a determined conquest of this thing between them.

"Rosa," he began, and stopped.

She almost laughed in his face, for she was suddenly struck with the absurdity of a pair of middle-aged people attempting to make love. No, it wasn't that, exactly, either.

She could still make love, all right, if the right person came along. But Ben Ortiz—and this time she did laugh.

Ben recoiled. "What's the matter, Rosa?"

Her laughter broke loose and filled the room. "Oh, nothing, Ben. I was just thinking—we used to do this without trying so hard. Remember?"

Ben looked a bit sheepish and nodded. Then he grinned. "We'd better have another glass of wine," he said, rising from his chair.

It was strong wine, new and rather bitter, but good on a cold night. The second glass untied their tongues. But Rosa was sad and filled with nostalgic memories. She couldn't charm a man any more, simply by looking at him in a certain way, and she would have liked to, to-night. The wine and the warmth and the strange surroundings brought a sweeping return of old and almost forgotten desires. It had been altogether too long since a man had looked at her with lust in his eyes. Was that, alas, entirely for the young?

She leaned toward Ben Ortiz, and he put his arm around her shoulders. Ah, that was almost right. She closed her eyes and imagined the rest.

They had another glass of wine before Rosa said she must go. It dulled the pain of realizing that old passions could not be recaptured. Ben had kissed her again, yes, but it wasn't like the old kisses. His arms could no longer encircle her as when she was slim and nimble. It was, in fact, more ludicrous than anything else to see him try.

"Well, Ben," she said, "it was good coming here. I had a nice time. Your wine is good, too. But I must go now."

"I'll walk back with you, Rosa."

On the way they spoke little. Rosa pulled her shawl tightly across her shoulders against the cold, and took short, quick steps. Ben strode beside her silently.

"Will you go back to the *baile*, Ben?"

"Yes, I think I'll go back for a while."

"I hope Juliano isn't too drunk. He thinks he's got to get drunk because José is home. I hope there won't be any trouble. You keep away from him, Ben, will you?"

"I'll try. Are you afraid for him—or for me?"

"For both of you."

Ben wouldn't risk a reply to this. He left Rosa at her house and walked down the road alone. She had drunk his wine, she had taken his kisses—what had she given him? Nothing. Nothing but a taste of bitterness. With his hands in the pockets of his overalls he trudged along the valley road, back to the *baile*. Afraid for him, was she? Ben laughed. She knew better than that—so did he. It was Juliano she was afraid for, the drunken, noisy fool. Well, she'd better be. One word out of that man to-night and Ben would show him.

Ben squared his shoulders and marched bravely under the stars, back to the *baile*, and stood in the doorway with his head high and his eyes defiant. Maybe he had a son who couldn't go to the war because he had a withered arm. Maybe he did. Well what of it? His eyes challenged every face they looked at—well, what of it? He could still stand on his own two feet. They couldn't make a fool or a sheep of Ben Ortiz just because his son couldn't go to the war. Those boys who had gone, and now come back, were no better than his boy—no better at all. Oh, they could talk English better, but see, how they laughed at their fathers now, and grinned impudently at the old people, and shook their heads as if they knew so much. He overheard a pair of them talking in the shadows of the wall outside, in Spanish, and one of them was the son of Juliano Trujillo, the prideful one.

"It's no good, coming back to this," one of them said. "There's nothing here for a man to do. Who wants to starve in the mud of these little fields? Dry up in this forsaken place?"

"Not me," the other rejoined, "you can't ever get anywhere in a place like this. No money, nothing to do. I'd rather be back in the army, wouldn't you?"

"Sure I would—back in the army. I'm going away as soon as I can get loose from my father."

"Where to?"

"Oh, up to Colorado—they need men for the mines up there, they say."

"Ah!" Ben turned away in disgust.

Men for the mines. Anything but work the land! Ben Ortiz smiled grimly. So that's what they went to war for—so they could come back and grub like prairie dogs in the earth—so they could dig all day in the black depths, and have money to spend. They had to have money to spend, did they? Was that what they learned at the war?

A withered arm. Cheap enough. But a sudden insane anger inflamed Ben Ortiz, not at anything in particular but at the ignorant stupidity of these men who boasted of sons like that who came home to ridicule and go away again. He felt like taking those two boys and knocking their heads together—he could do it, too, even though he hadn't been to war, even though his son had a withered arm.

Ben stood in the doorway, full of his wrath, tall, defiant, something like his old self.

If Juliano had come along just then with his drivel about a hundred Germans, Ben would have taken him by the throat and choked the stupid words out of him.

CHAPTER II

BEN hadn't many friends, any more. By his bitterness he had turned most of them away, and by his hermit-like solitude. But he felt reckless to-night, and more as he used to feel as a young man. He even danced a few times, and played his fiddle with the other musicians, took a few drinks. And he kept an eye on Juliano, and all the Trujillo brothers.

So did Beatriz, who was always worried when his brother got drunk, and fearful that he might start more trouble. Beatriz followed Juliano about to-night without letting his brother know it.

But he couldn't be with him all the time, and Juliano's raving seemed harmless enough. And he wasn't near when Juliano swayed through the doorway and came up face to face with Ben Ortiz.

"So it's you, is it? What's the matter with you, Ben Ortiz, that you send no sons to the war? Oho, my boy, José, he killed a hundred Germans——"

Ben gave Juliano a push that sent him back through the door outside, sprawled on the ground, and he went out after him, stood over him while Juliano got clumsily to his feet.

"You keep your mouth shut, Juliano," Ben warned fiercely.

"Why don't you send a son to the war, Ben? Maybe he's afraid to go, no? Maybe he's afraid, that boy of yours with the crooked arm! Haha."

Ben seized Juliano by the shoulders and shook him. "Be quiet, you——"

People were already beginning to fall away from them, standing in the light from the door. They were left alone in the centre of a watching circle of faces dimly visible, but the music inside prevented the dancers and others from hearing. Fantastic chorus to their hate.

Juliano stood up solidly on his legs, suddenly sobered. No swaying and blinking now. The two men faced each other, and Ben was shaking his clenched fist under Juliano's nose.

"You know very well why my boy didn't go to the war," he was saying, "and if you know what's good for you, you'll keep your mouth shut. I've taken enough from you."

"And I've taken enough from you, Ben Ortiz. I haven't forgotten what you did to me once. No, I haven't forgotten that. I saw you sneaking after her to-night. I know what kind of a pig you are!"

"Your wife is nothing to me. You're the pig, not me."

"You're a sneaking pig, and you've got a pig for a wife and a crippled pig for a son!"

Ben hit Juliano then with his fist on the side of the face, staggering him back into the shadows—but Juliano came on again muttering curses and raced into Ben with flaying arms. They grappled, fell, rolled on the ground. Ben had his knife out, first this time, and just then José, Juliano's soldier son, came out of the *baile* hall and dragged Ben Ortiz away. At his signal others came to help and the fight was stopped. Nobody seemed to have been hurt this time, but they took the two men home. Juliano raved as two of his sons, holding him by the arms, led him up the valley road, and they discovered that Juliano had blood on his hand.

"So, he cut you after all," said José. "Where?"

"He didn't hurt me. I'll kill him for this. I'll get that Ben Ortiz. He's done enough to me."

Yes, there was blood on his hand. Juliano fell asleep almost as soon as they got him on his bed, and then they took off his coat and found a gash in the fleshy part of the forearm. José put a bandage on it, and went back to the dance. They didn't know that Rosa was there ahead of them. She had been in another part of the house. She came in after they had gone and found Juliano lying on the bed asleep.

"Again," she muttered. "Ah, you idiots, men!"

Why must they always be fighting? She shook Juliano, trying to rouse him. "What was it this time? Juliano, Juliano! Wake up, tell me. Was it Ben Ortiz again? Was it?"

He rolled over and groaned, and she shook him harder. "Was it Ben Ortiz again?"

Without opening his eyes he grunted: "*Si—si—* Ben Ortiz. I saw him—following you——"

"Ah——" she let go of him with a push, and he flopped back on the pillow. "So he cut you did he? Well, it serves you right. Maybe it'll teach you not to be starting fights all the time."

No use trying to talk to Juliano. She stood over him and gritted her teeth. Ah, the fools. Why women ever had to do with men was more than she could see. How she used to lust after them, too, in the old days! Men, men, men. That was all she ever thought about. She shuddered, remembering. If she had known what she knew now, it would have been a different thing. This drunken lump of a man—think of lying with him all these years. Think of it!

She sat down beside the bed, and looked long and thoughtfully into Juliano's face, and she tried to remember what it was like to love. She couldn't remember. Had she never loved, then? Had it always been hate in disguise? Had she not loved Ben Ortiz when he came to her that night, that one night? She smiled with one side of her mouth only. No. No, she hadn't loved him—but she had loved what he gave her—she had loved that.

Why was that? What was the difference between her and little Nina? The same little Nina now as then, always loving, loving her husband or her children. Why, she didn't even love her children very much, did she? Except José. Him she had always adored. For a while she had loved the others, perhaps while they were young and needed her, while she could protect them, but now they were independent, like grown animals. Maybe if they had been another man's children——

Rosa stood up with a sigh and took off her clothes. Well, those days were gone. This misshapen body could never capture another man. She sighed as she blew out the lamp and got into the bed, first rolling Juliano over to one side where he belonged. Before she went to sleep she wondered if Ben Ortiz had been hurt in the fight.

CHAPTER III

JULIANO knew nothing until the next day when he awoke with an ache in his head and a much greater ache in his arm. They had to tell him all over again what had happened—and then he began to piece together odds and ends of memory and at last, lying in bed all day, he had the story in his mind by evening.

Oh, his arm was sore! But it was nothing—only a scratch, José said. He said other things, too. Why didn't Juliano go to law about it? There were such things as law in the land now, you know. He could have Ben Ortiz arrested and thrown into jail if he wanted to.

Juliano scoffed at such silly ideas. This was an affair between himself and Ben Ortiz. They knew how to handle it; they needed no law. They had got along for fifty years without going to law, and he guessed they could go on for the rest of their lives. But that Ben Ortiz had better look out—the next time he might not escape so easily.

"Did Ben get hurt in the fight?" Rosa asked. They were the first words she had spoken to Juliano.

And he turned on her wrathfully. "Hear how she asks about Ben Ortiz, when her husband is lying here with a cut on his arm! Ah, you're no good, you Rosa. You're no kind of a wife for a man. I saw you go off with him last night. I saw you!"

"Is that why you fought?" she asked calmly.

"No."

"Why, then?"

"I don't know. It was—something else."

And Rosa left his room without more words.

Juliano kept a rag around his wounded arm after he rose from his bed; but the pain never left it, never for an instant did it leave him in peace. For days the wound throbbed, although it appeared to be healing, and nobody thought much about it. He went out with the boys to cut wood, but on the day for taking it into the town to sell he couldn't go because his arm was hurting him so. They went without him, leaving him with Nina and Rosa. And before the boys returned Juliano was forced to return to his bed again, for he felt sick all over. And his arm throbbed like nothing he had ever felt before.

When they came back they found him groaning, with Rosa and Nina looking on helplessly. Rosa still was not much concerned. If a man must be sick, he must be sick, that was all. He would get well, or die.

José, however, looked at the wound. "It's bad," he said. "We've got to do something about it."

124

"What is there to do?" said Rosa. "He can't go to the town."

"We'll have to get him to the doctor. It's very bad."

Juliano snorted. "Doctor," he sneered with disgust. "I've never been to a doctor. I won't go to any doctor. Protestants! Bah!"

José shook his head. "What will you do, then?"

"Get *Dona* Maria. She knows what to do."

"Who?"

"*Dona* Maria Ortiz. But to-morrow. Leave me alone now. I want to sleep."

They left him alone. In the morning his arm looked more like a leg than an arm, a short, fat leg.

Dona Maria came. One of the younger boys went for her, and she came thumping over the road, up the hill to the Trujillo house. She was a tiny woman. She looked more like some kind of an aged, mischievous elf than a woman with four grown sons and a daughter, long since left her for other places. She didn't know where they were, nor did anyone else; and she didn't care. Rare among women she had achieved a fame of her own in the valley, feared somewhat, respected, consulted in all manner of troubles. She was midwife, doctor, counsel. And she wore a floppy old sack of a hat pulled down low over her eyes, under which her wild, straight locks of yellow grey hair hung down front and back, terrifying. She frightened children, and was used up and down the valley for that purpose, also.

"You be good, now, or I'll get *Dona* Maria after you!"

Dona Maria came and entered the house as if she owned it already. What fire that tiny body contained!

"Get out, all of you. It's no good, standing around and looking at him. Rosa, get me a clean cloth— Nina, some hot water. Rosa, make those boys go outside."

They left him to the women. Only José was sceptical, and dared to look upon *Dona* Maria with anything but awe. But José had been to the war. He knew a thing or two about wounds. He didn't like the look of this, and said so.

But his doubt availed nothing. *Dona* Maria took some herbs out of a dirty little sack she brought and brewed them on the stove. Marvellous! Nina and Rosa looked on with wonder. So competent, this mite of a woman with stringy hair! She took the bandage off Juliano's arm, clucked over it, threw it away. Then she bathed the wound in her concoction and put a clean bandage on it. It frightened the other women by its angry, swollen look, but *Dona* Maria was calm, always calm. And she went away again, but demanding her pay before she would leave the house.

"How much?" said José.

126

"Ten dollars."

"Ten dollars? Oh, it's too much, woman."

"Do you want him to die?"

"No, but——"

"Ten dollars, then. Hurry, I can't stand here all day."

They consulted, all of them—Beatriz, Cruz, José and the women. Between them they managed to raise five dollars and they gave it to *Dona* Maria, who accepted it and went away growling.

José was in a rage. "You pay that old woman five dollars for nothing. Nothing, I tell you! You'll see. He won't get any better."

Before the image of a saint painted on an old hand-hewn piece of wood, Rosa lighted a candle for Juliano's health. This she secretly believed more effective than *Dona* Maria, or any other treatment, for she believed in God. All of them, except José, murmured a prayer now and then through the day before Rosa's hopeful flame. And Juliano tossed in fever, and raved insanely. His arm was swollen three, four times its natural size while the family looked on helplessly, waiting, hoping for *Dona* Maria's magic to have effect.

Juliano grew worse. It was a neighbour, not one of the family, who first set loose the thought that the swelling of Juliano's arm was the work of a witch; and it was the same neighbour, unnamed, who named the witch. Rosa.

127

Swift the flight of the evil thought! By nightfall, through the length and narrow breadth of the valley, they had it that Rosa had bewitched her husband so she could get rid of him and marry Ben Ortiz. It came to the members of her family in due time, and they took in the thought, nourished it, found it plausible and commenced to cast their suspicions upon poor, guiltless Rosa.

For a long time she didn't even know what the trouble was, and saw their growing hostility with wonder. People avoided her, gave her angry looks, all the next day, and in the house it was the same, suspicion, angry, hateful glances. When she could bear it no longer she went to Beatriz because he was kind and she said: "What is it, Beatriz? Why does everybody look at me? What's the matter?"

But the soft eyes of Beatriz were not kind now. They were hard like the others. "Rosa," he said severely, "the people are saying that you've put a spell on him. You want to be rid of him. Is it true?"

"Mother of God, no, Beatriz! Oh, *por Dios*——!" And she went off wailing and wringing her hands.

"Rosa!" Beatriz called her back. "If you did do this—you must save him. You must take off the spell. The people are angry——"

"Oh, Beatriz—do you think—do you believe that I could do such a thing?"

Beatriz shrugged. "It looks bad, Rosa. His arm was

all right—then it began to swell. Somebody did it to him. They think it must be you." And Beatriz, the kind one, went suddenly cold all over and seized Rosa by the wrist. "You take the spell off Juliano", he growled between clenched teeth, "or the people will kill you!"

Rosa wrenched her wrists free of this icy grip. Her fear fled before a towering wrath and outrage.

"So", she snarled, "you're like them, too, Beatriz. I didn't think you were. Ah, Mother of God, how I hate you all. Stupid, stupid, superstitious, ignorant people! All of you! Everybody in this mean little valley! Witches, ghosts—you're afraid of your shadows! You'll kill innocent people because you're afraid of your shadows! Ah, you fools!"

She stood off from him with her hands on her hips, looking him up and down, scornfully. "You and your spells," she sneered. "What do I know about spells? And if I did, why should I want to get rid of Juliano? Do you think I want that Ben Ortiz?" She laughed crazily. "Well, I don't want him. I've had him, and I don't want him. You can tell him that, too. Tell your friends, tell the people who call me a witch. And tell them, too, that I hate every one of them, and I think they're all a pack of coyotes and fools. Tell them that, and see how they like it! If I could, I'd put a spell on the whole lot of them and send them howling down to hell!"

Rosa fled from the house after that, and Beatriz stood there frowning. But the frightened gleam in his eyes revealed that where he might have been in doubt before, he was certain now. She was a witch, all right. No woman could rant and scream like that, say such terrible things, unless she was inspired by the devil.

As her passion stilled, Rosa was frightened again, and she went to José with tears in her eyes. He put his arms around her and tried to comfort her. He hated them, too, those ignorant ones whose superstitions held over into a world of marvels. He had seen the marvels. He knew that everything had an answer and a cause. But they only made him feel that his knowledge was a taint in Vallecito.

"Never mind, mother—don't listen to them. They're only ignorant. They still believe in ghosts and witches, and there's nothing we can do about it. They'll forget about it; leave them alone and let them forget it."

"But why, José? What have I ever done that could make them say such a thing of me? I always laughed at it before, but now—they're serious. They might want to hurt me."

"Nobody will hurt you."

"But what are they saying, José? How did it get started? What have I ever done——?"

"I don't know. They don't talk in front of me.

They don't dare. They know that I'd cut their hearts out!"

She looked at him, and saw that he was hiding something. "No, José. Tell me, then. I'm not afraid."

José looked down at his shoes. "Well—it's hard to believe, what I heard. They've been blaming you, you know, for a lot of things—for a long time."

"For what?"

"Oh, for sickness, and——"

"But, José, how could they?"

"I don't know, damn their souls! They don't think —they just talk. There's a story going around——" He stopped, shaking his head.

"What story, José?"

"Oh, it's too crazy—like a child's bad dream."

"What story? Tell me."

"Well, somebody saw an owl——"

"An owl——?"

"Yes, an owl—and he threw a stone at it and hurt its wing. It fell to the ground—it was in a tree. And when the man tried to catch it, it ran away, down the road, and he followed it. He followed it all the way to—to our house here. It went in the door. He went in after it. And inside he found not the owl, but you, lying on the bed holding your arm, which you'd hurt some way——"

"But, José, it's a lie! It's all a lie!"

"Of course it's a lie. If I could find the man who told it——!"

"But what does it mean? Witches go around as owls? So I'm the witch. The owl came here—I see, now. How long have they been telling that story?"

"I don't know. I just heard it yesterday. It was told to me by one of the boys who came back with me. He thought it was funny—thought I ought to know about it. We're trying to find the man who started it."

"Oh, don't find him, José. What good will it do? Get you into trouble, that's all."

"If I find him, I swear I'll kill him! I'll carve his heart right out of him!"

"No, no, José! Let it go. It can't do any harm, really. It's just talk. The people are all mad. Why, I never hurt anybody in my life. I've helped them, in all kinds of ways. Maybe I've helped them too much."

José took charge, after this. No time could be lost. That night he took matters into his own hands and hitched up the team, laid a bed for Juliano in the body of the wagon and placed his father in it and started for the town. Two of his brothers and their uncle, Cruz, went with him.

It was near dawn when they clattered down the long hill into town, and nobody was abroad. José didn't know where to go and Cruz, who should have known, was at a loss because he hadn't kept track of the changes in the town through the war, fearful of being taken. They drove to the *plaza* and waited there for an inspiration while the horses drooped their heads almost to the pavement and went to sleep. At last they saw a man walking alone and José got down from the wagon and went to him.

"I've got a sick man—my father—in the wagon over there. We want a doctor."

"How sick?"

"Oh, very, very sick. He may die if we don't get him to a doctor quick."

"Better take him to the hospital. Come along, I'll go with you."

They took him in, after many questions, and laid him in a bed in a ward. The brother and sons stood downstairs in a disconsolate knot, while they waited for the doctor to come. At last he came. They waited and waited, endlessly. Then a sister appeared before them, whisking into the room silently all in white like an angel.

"The doctor says the arm must come off. He's going to operate right away."

Cruz made a movement to object, but José gripped his arm and stopped him.

The bells of the cathedral nearby tolled for early Mass.

CHAPTER IV

THE quick, right action of José had no effect, however, upon the madness which possessed Vallecito over Rosa's witchery. The persecution of her went on. It was a violent temper that held the people tensely—a tenuous thread that kept them from savage action.

Poor Rosa!

José and Cruz and the young men came home sadly with the news that Juliano was very low indeed and might not live. And they found Rosa red-eyed, beside herself with fear and weeping. José's anger was unlimited. Oh, that he should live in a place as mad as this! Powerless, he was, too; powerless to help or change them at all. Then he had an idea—the priest was due in the valley on the coming Sunday. He would go to him and make him preach to the people about the folly of believing in witches, and of persecuting a poor woman whose only guilt was a readiness to help her neighbours.

José could hardly believe what he saw. Wherever a sun-warmed adobe wall faced the south along the valley road a group of people gathered there and talked; and whenever José or a member of his family went by they stopped and stared as if a plague were passing. He tried to act unconcerned and natural, but they wouldn't let him. If he joined a group they fell silent and edged away from him, for they knew he opposed their belief and considered him as guilty as Rosa. Could it be that such madness lived in a world where men had conquered the land and the sky and the waters? Could human souls be still so black? Oh, how he hated those people now! His poor mother shivering in the lonely hiding of her innocence, not daring to show herself abroad, trembling day and night—— Ah, God punish them!

He stalked up and down the valley road, defying the whispering knots of men, trying to show them his defiance, his contempt, letting them see that he, at least, would stand for no nonsense.

Yes, he was afraid somebody might still stir them to violence, not because they cared so much about Juliano, but because they hated and feared a witch. It was not the young men, he discovered—they were only amused by the whole fever of stupidity—but the older people, Juliano's contemporaries, who were making the trouble. No, the young people couldn't believe in witches, not with the new school in the valley and automobiles everywhere on the roads and moving pictures and marvels of all kinds to undeceive them. José told them that if a man got blood poisoning in his arm it would swell, and no witch could have anything to do with it, even if there were such things as witches. And they believed him; he was something of a hero in their eyes, anyway, having been to the war and seen many things they could never hope to see.

José hoped to counteract the temper of the older people by setting the young against them, until the priest should come and give them all a lacing in the church.

Meanwhile, Rosa huddled shaken in her house, fearful even of the light of day. José was the only one who believed in her perfect guiltlessness, for even Beatriz and Cruz and Nina eyed her with unconcealed suspicion. So she feared them as well. And she begged José not to leave her alone in the house.

Saturday came. The others of the family were in the town to see Juliano, and Rosa was alone with José, and she felt secure for the first time since Juliano was taken away. They sat together in the *placita* in the afternoon, for spring was not far off and it was warm in the sun. And the priest would come to-morrow and would quiet the whole affair. José consoled his mother with such assurances, until sundown when they had to go in out of the cold. Down the road they could hear the music from the *baile* hall where another dance was going on, but they sat quietly in the house relishing the peace of it. And when José went outside to get wood for the fire he looked down the road and saw a group of people coming towards the house. He waited until he saw them turn in at the gate and start up the knoll.

Then he went inside and told his mother.

"Some people are coming," he said as gently as he could, but she jumped to her feet and began to tremble and clasp her hands. José's heart contracted to see her so overwrought.

"Come, mother. We'll go away until they've gone."

"No—let them come, José. I don't care——"

"All right. I'll go out and stop them."

He took a gun with him—the old one belonging to Juliano that his father had left him—and waited, seated on the doorstep with the gun across his knees.

The men came on, entered the *placita* and looked around, cautiously.

"What do you want?" said José from the door.

"Who's that?"

"What do you want here?" José repeated.

A man came forward from the group. It was Ben Ortiz.

"What do you want, Ben Ortiz?"

Ben sneered. "Oh, it's you. Where is she?"

"Where is who?"

"That woman—that witch. Your mother."

137

"She's inside," said José. "What do you want with her?"

The others had come up now and stood about in a circle with their eyes on the rifle in José's hands. The boy stood in the doorway, blocking it.

"We came to get her—run her out of the valley," said Ben more thoughtfully now, considering the rifle. "Stand aside."

José laughed. "The first man who tries to get past this door is dead," he said evenly. "And you, Ben Ortiz, you'd better get out of here before I get mad and kill you, anyway."

They stepped back a few paces. José's heart was jumping wildly but he stood his ground, his finger on the trigger of the old rifle. And then, as deliberately as they had come, the men turned about and walked away.

José, as he sank weakly to the doorstep, was filled with a fresh contempt for them. Cowards! Coyote-hearted idiots!

"They've gone," he told his mother, who was cringing in the darkest corner of the room. "They won't dare come back." Then he laughed contemptuously. "They're afraid, you know."

"Who were they?" Rosa whispered.

"Oh, I don't know—just a bunch of men from the *baile*—half drunk. They went back quick enough when they saw the gun."

138

He laughed again and hung the rifle on its hook over the bed. Rosa came out of the corner and sat down in a chair, pale and shaken. "Oh, Mother of God, when will this end? Why do they think I did such a thing? Why, José? Why?"

"Because they're fools and haven't any sense. They'll forget all about it after to-morrow. You'll see."

The youthful, the hopeful José! He little knew how well the people could remember some things which they didn't want to forget.

"No," said Rosa hopelessly, "they won't forget. You don't remember, José—but I do. There was a woman in the valley before, when I was a girl. Everybody said she was a witch. We were all afraid of her—we children ran away when we saw her. And she was blamed for everything that happened, because they said she had the evil eye. People wouldn't let her into their houses. She lived all alone —until she died."

"Oh, that was in the old days, mother. It can't be like that any more."

José was partly right. It wasn't as bad as it was in the old days, but for Rosa it was bad enough.

The priest told the people in the church on Sunday that they were doing wrong to believe in witches. He scolded and raged at them and made them angry, and it quieted their active hatred. But a delegation

139

went into the town later and asked the church authorities there to give them a different priest in Vallecito, because the one they had, told them they mustn't believe in witches.

Nothing came of it, except another rebuke to the delegation. And then, when they heard that Juliano would live, was getting well, they forgot about Rosa for the present, or assumed that she had repented.

CHAPTER V

"I'LL never feel comfortable with any of the valley people again," Rosa had said to José.

"Oh, yes, mother. They'll be coming around again like they did before, asking you to help them. You'll see."

And Rosa remembered this. It was true, too. Very soon people began appearing at the Trujillo house: breathless boys and girls begging Rosa to come on the run and help with a baby that was coming, or to soothe a fever with her wonderful hands.

Rosa began to feel alive again, but something was different still. She tired easily. She wasn't the same energetic woman who could work a whole day without feeling it, and be ready to work half the night as well. She thought little of it, though, told herself she was getting old.

Some families in the valley had always been poor. They were the ones whose fields were already too small, whose men were shiftless or lost to drink. Rosa felt deeply for these families, though she despised them as individuals, especially the men. They were always coming to her for one thing and another, sending their ragged little children to her with a plea for this and that. She couldn't resist the wide-eyed appeal in their eyes, though she well knew they were little beggars at heart, to the manner born.

She always went. And when on a day a week or so after the traitorous Ben Ortiz had come to steal her away, a child knocked timidly on her door and said, "Please, *Senora*, my sister is sick and my mother wants you to come," she went, as usual.

The house was one she knew, a poor, poor place far down the valley where the pinching hills all but smothered the farming lands. One room and a dirt floor, but white walls, kept spotlessly white always. It was not as clean as it looked, however. As she sat by the bed where the child lay she saw lice crawling on the wood of the bed frame, and she shuddered in spite of herself. Chicken-lice, they were. They had some scrawny chickens scratching in the baked earth outside the door, and they came in and out of the room like members of the family, and scratched absurdly on the hard dirt floor. Rosa shooed them out before she did anything else, but there was nothing she could do about the lice on the bed; except keep clear of them herself.

And as she sat there beside the bed, stroking the hot forehead and talking in low, soothing tones to the child, she noticed that the room began to fill with people. At first she thought little of it, assumed that they were relatives, come to see the child, and then she began to be alarmed. Something else was in the air. The child was not very ill, a fever from a poor little stomach overburdened with bad food. She pretended not to notice the thickening hostility behind her, continued to stroke the child's forehead calmly.

But the intense, hateful power of a dozen eyes pressed upon her from behind. Her heart began to contract, as if the forces of hatred squeezed it with cold fingers. Her breath came quickly and sweat stood on her forehead. Meanwhile she talked in low tones to the girl on the bed, and thought swiftly of what she should do. What could she do? She was caught, trapped in the circle of their eyes.

She decided at last that she should try to leave, and she stood up. She was met by the full force of their combined, withering stare. For a moment she held her own against it—then, beaten, her eyes fell to the floor and a panic swept her. Summoning all her courage she raised her head again and said, "The child will be all right. Give her some milk if you can, goat's milk. You have goats?"

One of the men nodded.

"And don't let her have any coffee for a while, or beans." As she spoke, Rosa had an eye on the door, and when she finished, she started for it.

A man stepped into her way, stopping her. She

143

looked at him questioningly while her heart throbbed.

"Wait," the man said. "Did you take the spell off her?"

"Spell——?" Rosa gasped.

"Yes. You put a spell on her. You'll take it off, or——"

Rosa was frightened now, all right. "I—I don't know what you mean," she faltered.

"Oh, yes, you do." He pointed at the girl on the bed. "She told us about it, before she got sick."

"About what?"

The man sniggered brutally. "I guess you know, all right. Well, will you take the spell off her?"

Rosa bit her lip; she was trembling; she looked down at the floor, swept the semicircle of faces without hope. If she only knew what they thought she had done, she might carry the thing through in their own tempo, in their own way.

"What did she say—the little girl?"

The man hesitated, stared searchingly into her face as if to see written there the tale of the lie which he thought her black heart contained. "She said", he began like the voice of judgment, "that you spoke to her the other day, and that after she had gone by you picked something up off the ground and kept it. When she got home, her hair-ribbon was gone."

He turned and pointed dramatically at the child.

"Now she's got the fever. And you did it. You've got to take it away!"

Rosa's heart skipped. All of it was quite possible, plausible, even. Any or all of it might easily have happened—except for the hair-ribbon. She had no hair-ribbon. Lacking anything else to say, she said that. "I have no hair-ribbon. What—what if I can't take her fever away?"

"You can. You will."

Rosa shuddered visibly. For a moment hot anger rose to her throat, but fear possessed her now. She could only think of what immediately to do, not of how she loathed these superstitious people. And terror crept back and seized her stealthily. She stammered through her chattering teeth. "I—I don't know what to do. What do you want me to do?" She spread her arms helplessly to the whole group, looking at each in turn, opening her countenance wide for them to see.

They saw no innocence there, though. The hard lines of their faces held. "Take the spell off our daughter," growled the man who had first spoken. "We know what you are. *Bruha!* Witch! First you try to kill your husband—then you try to hurt our little girl. But we won't let you do it! We'll keep you here until you take the spell off her, no matter what. Well. Will you do it? Or will we beat you until you do?" He even raised a threatening arm to her.

Rosa stepped back, her hand at her mouth. Thought came slowly to her rescue; her brain began to race along possible ways. If José should hear of this—no, he must not. He might do anything in his fury. She must guard him from himself, handle this thing by her own ingenuity. She felt a crafty calm coming over her, and her mind cleared. The child wasn't very ill—she might be able to fool them into thinking she had made her well. Only one hindrance to that, though; if she did that, they'd be sure she was a witch, ever after. And so would the rest of the valley. The word would go about that Rosa had lifted a spell off a little girl. And that would be the end. The end! Never any peace again. Never. Nothing but hatred, suspicion, loathing.

Horror-struck, she cast about for another way. She could make a break for freedom, run for it. No chance. The men would catch her haul her ingloriously back again. Ah, poor Rosa! So this was the end of her good works! She wanted to cry with self-pity, with desperation of being at last at her wits' end. The people were to win at last, then, and crucify her on the cross of their stupidity. She hung her head, overpowered by the bitterness of it. No, there was no other way.

Raising her face to them she said in a voice so thin that they could scarcely hear it: "Very well, then— I'll take the spell off. But you must leave me alone

with the little girl. And remember—if you watch, that
will spoil it, and it won't work."

She didn't know why she said that—merely to add
to the mystery, she supposed. Certainly all she could
do could be seen without effect, one way or another.
But they took her very seriously and with sidelong
glances filed out of the house. Warnings spoke from
their glittering eyes.

Left alone with the child, Rosa sat down again
beside her and pondered what to do. There was
nothing to do. She had no medicines to give it. If
in some way she could empty that languishing stomach of all it contained—but how? Oh, she knew a
few simple remedies—most of the people did. But did
she dare to use them? Suppose the child should get
worse instead of better? Well, that was the chance
she'd have to take. Searching the cupboards, she
found the ingredients of an emetic, mixed it, and fed
it to the girl. Though it was somewhat heroic for the
patient, it might have the right effect; and before
anything happened she called the people in.

They came quickly; they had not been far off.

"She'll be sick to-night," Rosa told them. "She'll
throw off the poison in her stomach. To-morrow
she'll be all right again. Now may I go?"

The man who had done the talking considered the
child carefully for a while, consulted with the others
in the room in undertones. They nodded to each

other at last, one of them mumbled that the girl looked better already. "Yes, you may go. But if she doesn't get better, we'll come after you again."

Their angry eyes followed her as she left the house. She felt them boring into her back as she walked up the road.

So. Now she was a witch, by her own admission. She wasn't afraid of them any longer, nor of what they might do. Not with José in the house. She could almost laugh to think what José would do to them if they should come back for her. She'd have to tell him then, but she could make light of it and keep him from getting angry. A man who had been to the war knew too much about guns and killing. She'd have to be very careful.

She smiled to think what was happening back there in that house now, with the child puking all over the place, and the people cursing her. Let them curse! Precious harm it could do. Animals. Animals! That's what they were. No more brains than cows. Was she to be blamed, then, every time one of their stomachs revolted? The injustice of it, the idiocy, made her boil, now that her personal danger was past. As she hurried up the road to her house she gave herself completely to a white-heat of rage, not only upon those people but upon all people like them; upon the valley, the inhuman hills, the little mean life they enclosed.

She arrived at her house with her passion spent and a great exhaustion in her body. Throwing herself on her bed, she closed her eyes and let the vortex of feelings in her heart seethe, simmer and subside.

She lay there so long that the others of the family, coming in after the day's work, thought she was ill. And in fact she was ill. She felt drained, and she had a pain in her side. She got up and dragged herself through the evening, helping Nina with the cooking, but she hardly spoke and her face was a mask turned inwards, with nothing showing except holes for her eyes, her nose, her mouth.

José sought her out after supper.

"Something's the matter, mother. What is it?"

"Nothing, José. I'm tired, that's all. I went down there to that Sanchez house, and—oh, everything's so poor down there. They have so little to eat. The children are all sick and ragged—the chickens come in and leave lice in the house. They live like animals. Animals!"

José took her hand and held it, patting it gently. "I know. Some of the people here would be better dead. All dead. It's terrible. But there's something else, isn't there? You don't seem well."

"No. Only——"

"Only what?"

"Only this pain in my side. It comes and goes. It's pretty bad to-night. It's because I'm tired."

"What is the pain? What causes it?"

"Oh, it isn't anything. It's just because I'm tired."

She was lying. The pain, lately, was always there, sometimes bad, sometimes light, but always enclosing her in its four relentless walls.

She went to bed early.

The news was not long in spreading up and down the valley. The Sanchez girl had been cured by Rosa Trujillo. She had come and taken her spell off her. She was a witch, then, sure enough. People had better watch out for her.

José heard it, and came storming to his mother with the tale. She laughed. It was nothing. She made light of it. She had gone down there and found the child sick with a stomach full of beans and chilli and coffee. She had given her an emetic, and it had worked. That was all. José must think no more of it. Must forget it.

But José did no forgetting. For a day he brooded about it, considering all measures from murder to tolerance, and resolved at last to go down there, at least, and have his say. As a man who had been to the war he was respected in the valley; and as a man of parts somewhat feared. The next evening at sundown he walked to the Sanchez house, and in his heart he was prepared for anything. He was not armed. Purposely, to guard against his temper, he had left all weapons at home, even his knife. But in his hands, in his fists, he had all the power of an accumulated hatred.

Six or seven boys and girls were playing before the house, dirty-faced, unkempt, ragged. He took one by the shoulders, a boy, and held him firmly.

"Which of you was sick?" he said.

The boy pointed to his sister, playing in a pool of mud. José went to her. "How do you feel to-day?"

"I feel all right," she said in a frightened, thin little voice.

"What was the matter with you?"

"I was sick."

"I know, but why?"

Her eyes opened wide. "Oh, that woman—that witch—she put a spell on me!"

"But don't you know," said José angrily, "that there's no such thing as a witch? All you had was a belly-ache."

"Oh, no. My papa said it was that woman. He made her make me well, too."

José choked back his anger; and in its place came a great welling hopelessness, poignant as a sob. He turned about and walked away from the house, back to his home.

CHAPTER VI

JULIANO was getting well. They brought him back to
the valley as soon as he could be moved because they
couldn't pay the hospital for taking care of him, and
Juliano lay on his bed in the Trujillo house for weeks
and thought long about his missing left arm. He
winced whenever he remembered that the whole
thing had started over an arm—a withered arm. Now
he had no arm at all. Ben Ortiz got his revenge this
time, all right, perfectly. Oh, how he must be laughing! Juliano saw Ben in his dreams, grinning like a
fox over his triumph, and he would wake up with a
fury of hatred on him. And then when he could leave
his bed, the thought still haunted him and left him
with a feeling of impotence that was hard to abide.

His arm was gone—no power on earth could bring
it back—and it was as if Ben Ortiz had taken it from
him, stolen it. That was a terrible thing, to steal a
man's arm, for he needed two arms to work the land
and to cut the wood to sell in the town. It would be
different if Juliano were an old man who had no
more need of his arms any more, but here he was only
fifty-three with one arm gone.

They fixed a place for Juliano to sit in the *placita* on warm days and from there he could survey his fields and his family like a king. He saw a change in Rosa—they hadn't told him yet about all the agitation over her witchcraft. She seemed more subdued, and that was only fitting. He took it to be concern over his illness. And he was glad to see some show of affection after all these years. Oh, he had tamed the wild girl at last! Look at her now, meekly doing his bidding, silent, humble. No more bossing, no more rages and scenes. It was good, good.

Yes, Juliano was the master of his household now. While he was still sick and in some pain he made them all wait on him and attend to every wish and whim. Only José was sullen and discontented, and this puzzled the father somewhat, until he called him over to his place in the *placita* one day and spoke to him about it.

"What's the matter with you, José? Don't you like to be home again after the war? Maybe you like the army better than this, no?"

"No. They haven't told you—but while you were away, the people here in the valley made lots of trouble for us."

"Who made trouble?" said Juliano, roused to quick anger.

"All the people—except the young ones, they knew better."

"What do you mean? What kind of trouble?"

"They said that—mother—had put a spell on you, made your arm swell up. They even came up here to the house one night to—to take her away."

Juliano growled in his throat, but he couldn't speak because he was remembering something. He narrowed his eyes and looked off along the hills. "A witch——" he muttered. "*Bruha.*" Then he looked hard at José. "And what happened then?"

"I stopped them. I took your old gun and scared them off."

"Who were they?"

"I don't know. It was night—I couldn't see. I was too scared to notice, anyway, except for the one I talked to."

"Who was he?"

"Ben Ortiz."

"So. Ben Ortiz, again." He was silent for a time, while his eyes resumed their aimless searching of the hills. "A witch is a bad thing," he said reflectively.

"Ah," José interposed with savage disgust, "there's no such thing as a witch! What's the matter with these people? They're all mad! You got blood-poisoning in your arm, from the cut in your arm—it swelled up—they had to cut it off or you would have died. Witch! God damn them for stupid burros! I saw it every day in the army. Nobody talked of witches there. A fine thing that would have been—

to wait around for a witch to come and take off her spell! If anybody's a witch around here it's that *Dona* Maria, with her funny hat and her evil eyes!"

Juliano looked at his son with a mixture of admiration and disapproval. He smiled a little—the young were forever so, doubting the wisdom of their elders. Maybe they had no witches in France, but in Vallecito—yes, he had seen them with his own eyes—seen their devilish works, too. He twitched, and looked down at the stump of his arm. "You know—it's a funny thing—sometimes I get a pain in my hand there—and I look down—and my hand isn't there."

José grunted, in no mood to change the subject so easily. He stood up to leave his father. "Well, they'd better leave her alone. I may get mad and—and hurt somebody if they don't."

Juliano watched José as he walked away. It was all right. He wanted to be alone, to think this thing out. How many times he had thought the same thing about Rosa! That smile, that quick, piercing look in her eyes, always laughing, laughing, when there was nothing to laugh at. It was a thing to puzzle a man. He felt a stab of remorse, realizing that he might very well have started the whole thing himself, by calling her a witch that night before all the people. Too bad. He meant her no such harm. He was drunk, and his secret thoughts came out. But how did he know she didn't put a spell on him? How did he know that?

And he resolved to make an ancient test of witches, out of a vague remembrance in the back of his mind. Wasn't it said in the old days that a witch could never pass a crucifix? Yes, that was it. That was it. He'd make the test, just out of curiosity; just to appease a gnawing doubt. . . .

When he went into the house he took an old crucifix which had stood on the mantel over the corner fireplace for many years and laid it on the floor beside the doorsill. Then he called for Rosa. She came to the door and stood just outside the threshold, with her hands on the frame, peering into the gloom inside.

"Did you call, Juliano?"

"Yes, Rosa—come inside."

"What is it? I'm busy."

"Come inside a minute, Rosa."

As she stepped through the doorway, her heel touched the crucifix and she felt the unevenness, looked down. She stooped to pick up the little cross, stood in the doorway holding it in her hand, looking at Juliano. "Why, what's this doing on the floor? It belongs——"

Then she caught the fiendish glower in Juliano's eyes. "Ah," she cried in a long, despairing sigh which contained the flight of the last vestige of hope. "You, too, Juliano! You believe them, too." Her hands drooped to her side and she swayed so perilously that Juliano started from his chair as if to catch her when she fell. But she caught the frame of the door and held herself steady while she dropped her head to the crook of her arm and stood thus, a picture of despair.

Juliano's heart softened. He was sorry for what he had done. Ah, if he could only foresee the consequences of his deeds! But no, he was not the foreseeing kind. That was why he was so often sorry afterwards for things he had done. He looked at Rosa, standing distraught in the door, limp as a shrivelled cornstalk, and as lifeless. Yes, he was sorry.

And she had not passed the crucifix. Did he know any more, then, for all his trouble, for all the pain he had caused? A witch cannot pass a crucifix. But she would have passed it if she hadn't stepped on it—wouldn't she? Oh, surely she would!

His heart cried out to her, out of memories of the past. Rosa, Rosa, I die for love of you!

But his lips were silent and his mouth held its saturnine droop. Occasionally his lips twitched, as words to say came to his tongue and died there, for lack of means to pass his lips. Never since the first days had he felt as tenderly towards his Rosa—and never had he been so powerless to express any of it. Why, why? Had he lost the knowledge of how to speak tenderly to her? Do all men lose it at last?

Before he could gather his mangled wits, she was gone, taking the crucifix with her. He even watched her go in silence. She dropped the arm that held her head, turned about with an infinite weariness in every move and vanished from his sight.

Juliano sat on alone. She had known his trick, guessed it quicker than a proper fiend. For this may he be damned!

Juliano shrugged, raising his eyebrows. The mood of remorse passed quickly. José was right about it, he guessed. José ought to know. He'd been to the war and seen the world. Perhaps they were behind the times in Vallecito—the old men, at least, like himself. It was hard to erase old memories, old fixed ideas. A man could hardly be blamed——

Innocent or not, Rosa was his old love and his first love. Innocent or not, her repentance must now be complete. Yes, he would try to be kind to her from now on. And he would defend her, most of all from that cowardly Ben Ortiz, who turned against her when she was down. He would defend anybody, friend or enemy, against that man now. Anybody!

And soon there was no more time for thinking. Spring was upon them; the ditch had to be cleared of a winter's debris and collapse, and all the men in the valley gave a day's time to it.

The land again, the land! When the land called, all human things gave way, and it was only right that they should. For a man's fate lay in his fields, not in his heart; and the land was exacting of a man, too.

It demanded his best efforts and all his strength. Rightly so.

Juliano raged at his awkwardness with one arm, worked like a fiend trying to manage a shovel with it, and periodically flung the spade down and stood up and cursed the air dark with imprecations upon his clumsiness and Ben Ortiz. That first day of work was a nightmare and a madness of frustration. The shovel defeated him, tipped the dirt out of itself and refused to do his bidding until he could have torn it into pieces in his wrath. It became the symbol of his misfortune, and a crafty imp tormenting him.

Juliano came home exhausted, discouraged, chastened, but grimly determined. He never realized the importance of two arms before. And his remaining arm was sore, aching in every muscle. In the morning he didn't see how he could use it at all, but he drove himself to it, and practised swinging an axe with it at the wood-pile. At first he couldn't even hit the mark his eye selected on the wood. Gradually, he noticed, his aim grew better, and the better it got the harder he worked, and the quips flew. He held the wood dangerously with his foot, risking the amputation of that member as well, and worked feverishly, heartened by every accurate blow. It would be a long time, though, before he would work instinctively with one arm, without inadvertently reaching out with the stump of the missing one to hold something with his left hand.

Juliano was driven by thoughts of Ben Ortiz and his son. A man with a withered arm was no good as a soldier—but still he could learn to do a number of useful things if he had the will. He might even learn to shoot with one arm.

Beatriz had bought a small rifle once for one of his boys, and Juliano borrowed this and went off alone into the hills to hunt rabbits with it. These lonely trips became a boon to him, for in the time it took to get out of the valley, and roam among the folded hills he was able to think much about a one-armed man in a two-armed world. At first he was deeply forlorn, easily robbed of hope, but slowly he began to see what could be accomplished with only one hand and his courage returned little by little.

He was utterly helpless with the gun at first. The muzzle swayed like a windy reed when he took aim, and his shots went wild. He shot at anything that presented a fair target, stones, twigs, anthills. And he cursed when the puffs of dust told him how far he had missed the mark. He never saw anything on these tours of the hills—he couldn't even tell where he had been when he came home, always empty-handed. When he wasn't thinking, he was shooting, with a kind of terrible concentration.

This preoccupation lasted most of the summer—

until one day he came home with a rabbit, plumped it triumphantly down on the table in the kitchen where Rosa and Nina were working, and stood off staring at it like a boy with his first prey. But he didn't tell them how he had only wounded it, and killed it with a stick

They laughed at him, and he grinned. After that he turned to other things and his humour improved. He worked in the fields, harder than anybody else, and another test came when the alfalfa had to be cut. They tried to discourage him from using a scythe, but he spurned their caution and went out alone with no one but the old dog trailing him; and no one saw his first agonizing attempts to swing a scythe with one arm. Agonizing they were, all right. He sat down at the edge of the field and almost wept, for he couldn't make the thing behave at all. And the dog flopped beside him, panting and rolling sentimental eyes at the master. Juliano, talking aloud, let it be known to the old dog how bitter he felt.

"Ah, Diamond," he said in a shaky voice, "it's no good. He's beaten me, I guess, that Ben Ortiz. He's beaten me this time." He wiped the sweat from his face, and rubbed the stump of his arm. "I need that old arm, Diamond—I need it bad."

And then when he had caught his breath and rested a bit, he thought again of the only thing that would ever redeem his lost confidence, to do everything with one arm that he had done before with two—and do it as well as before. Only that would ever satisfy him, that he could flaunt in the face of Ben Ortiz.

He rose and went back to the field and swung his scythe time and again in open ground to get the hang of it and the feel of balance in his arm. It still wobbled out of control. Then he tried tucking the butt-end of the handle under the stump of his left arm. There, that was better—the strokes were shorter, but he could guide the blade. After practising this for half an hour, he looked back upon what he had done, and he felt almost jubilant. No one could tell that it wasn't the work of a whole man. So, then. One more triumph. One more.

On the way home he counted up the conquests yet to be made. Loading a burro, harnessing a horse, tying a shoe—and shoeing a horse, milking a cow, and managing a hoe, a spade, a team of horses. Enough to keep a man busy with his one arm. Oh, yes— plenty. But he was grinning when he returned to the house, and they knew the work had pleased him.

For Juliano's moods these days were always trace- able to his success or failure at some new task, done with one arm. The others admired his courage, his will; and some even expressed surprise and wondered at this new-found determination. Other men would have resigned, given up. Juliano was old enough to quit and let his sons and brothers do the work, and he had an excuse for it, too. But they saw something driving him on and on, and wondered. He seemed to have more energy than before, when there had been nothing remarkable about him.

"What's come over you, Juliano?" Rosa said to him one day. "You work all the time now. Maybe you should rest a little. You're not young any more."

And Juliano looked at his wife and didn't answer her for a long time. Once in the middle of his staring silence he scowled and said:

"You thought I was finished after that, no?" He laughed harshly at her. "No, I'm not finished yet. You'll see. I'll do the work of a man. I'll do the work of two men." He laughed again, in the same way. "It takes more than a crazy man's knife to stop Juliano Trujillo!"

CHAPTER VII

WITH so many men ready to work on the Trujillo fields, the harvest was in quickly and Juliano's help was not needed at all. He worked with them, however, and as hard as any man—harder, really, because of his missing arm. And they treated him like an equal, pretending not to notice his awkwardness. It kept his spirits up.

But when the work was done, time lay heavily upon the place and Juliano was restless. The whole family suffered for it, especially Rosa. He seemed to delight in persecuting her, as if doing so relieved his ill-temper. He had been gentle with her for a while after the abortive episode of the crucifix; but his tenderness had quickly worn thin and now it was as if he had never doubted that she was a witch and a dangerous woman to have around.

He would call her over to his place in the *placita* and for no reason at all he'd say: "Aha, Rosa," with a leer, "you creep around here like a cat. What's the matter with you? Maybe you're a bad woman, no? *Quien sabe?*"

And sometimes Rosa would fight back, and then

another time she would find it not worth the trouble; but little wonder that she came to look upon Juliano with a special kind of loathing which had the death of love in it.

She gave up her visits to the sick and ailing and the chronically pregnant women in the valley whom she used to see regularly. She feared another scene like the Sanchez one, which cost her so much in freedom and peace of mind. When people came now, as they did occasionally, to say that she had put a spell on a member of their family, she laughed in their faces and threatened them with the faithful José. But she could see that her presence there was becoming a liability, cutting off the Trujillo family even from the impoverished intercourse of the valley. And she began to entertain thoughts of flight. They wouldn't have her in their houses anyway, now; and with José so ready to defend her they simply stayed away from the place.

She knew that she was ill with some deep malady. She thought, however, that some good years were left to her still, and she longed for a chance to live them in peace, away from this tight little community where she was universally feared or hated.

She said to José one day: "I've heard you say that you want to leave Vallecito."

"Yes. But not as long as they make your life an evil thing. I think you need me here, mother."

"What if we should go away together, José?"

His face brightened as he looked at her. Obviously he hadn't thought of it before. "We could do that, couldn't we?"

"Where did you mean to go?"

"To Colorado. To the mines." He grasped her hands in an access of enthusiasm. "We could go, mother. We could get out of here! You and I! Why don't we?"

"It's bad, dangerous work, José. I wouldn't like to think of you working in the mines."

"Oh, it's nothing. It's good pay. Five dollars a day."

"I know, but—I don't want to be a burden on you always, either, José. You must marry and have a family."

"Oh," he laughed, "there's time enough for that. I'm still young. And I'd like to do it for you. I'd like to get you out of here!"

She looked away sadly. "I'm no good here any more. I can't do anything. The people won't have me in their houses. Your father—even your father is afraid of me."

"God damn him!" José cried bitterly in English. "The old fool!"

"Hush, José. He's your father."

He looked at her in surprise. "You understood what I said?"

"No. But I could tell by the way you said it that it was wrong of you."

"But, mother, you might find work you could do up there. And until you did we could live on my pay. You're so wonderful with your hands."

"Yes, it's possible. I'm—not as strong as I used to be, though." She looked away again and her eyes dimmed. "I could come back here to die. I'd like to do that."

José in his youth shunned the thought of death. "To die?" He laughed uncomfortably. "But you're not going to die. Not for a long time."

"Who knows?" she sighed, suddenly remote from her son.

"Come, mother—let's do it. Soon!"

"Well—I'll be thinking about it, José."

It was a dry winter, almost no snow, and snow was vital to the earth. As he watched his mother wither under the unhappiness of her burden, José felt increasing impatience and bitterness. He couldn't stay in this place! But for her he would have left it long ago. Nobody seemed to care what happened to her. All they ever talked about now was the weather and when would it snow, and how would they be able to plant in the spring if it didn't snow? You can't plant seeds in dry soil—it's no good doing that. Oh, why didn't it snow?

And José didn't care whether it snowed or not. He

didn't feel a part of the land any more—something had uprooted him. If his mother should die—he had mysteriously had it on his mind since that day they talked about going away together—that would be the end for him. He'd never feel another tie to Vallecito. He'd have to go away and never see the place again.

Meanwhile he waited, watching her. Now and then he reminded her of their talk. But she seemed to be waiting for something, too, something so deeply buried in her heart that she couldn't share it with him.

He never discovered what it was, but on a day in February, after the Christmas season had passed with gentleness dominant, at last she came to him and said: "I'm ready to go now, José."

He was ready, too, as he had been for months. "Good," was all he said.

And they laid their plans. Rosa quietly got her belongings together, at times when the house was empty, and secreted them all in an old chest. She moved with a great tranquillity upon her, dreamlike, as if some great crisis had come and passed. What it was was simple enough, though she could not impart it to another soul. She had decided that she was not loved; that beneath the harsh and intemperate humour of her husband was no love. She had searched with minute care, and found none.

So now she was ready to go. Nobody needed her

here. They had enough money between them to get to the railroad and to buy tickets to a point in Colorado where the railroad ended and the mines were not far off. Rosa had saved for years against such an emergency, never dreaming that it would be just like this, and José had a little he had managed to put away.

They left without telling anyone where they were going. A friend of José took them by wagon to a tiny settlement in the valley of the *Rio Grande*, where another friend drove them in an ancient automobile to a station on the railroad. For Rosa it was an adventure scarcely touched with sadness; for José it was unmixed joy. Rosa had never ridden on a train before. The experience of sliding effortlessly over the land, of watching objects by the side of the way swim silently past the windows was thrilling and marvellous. The train was in fact a labouring, undersized relic of a thing which chugged up incredible inclines, dipped and swayed over range after range of pine-covered mountains. And its progress was halting and uncertain. But it was all new to Rosa, and all wonderful. She forgot the pain in her side.

At the end of the line, at a place called Antonito, she sent her message to Juliano. "I am leaving Vallecito for a while, until the people forget to hate me. I am not needed by any of you now, but some day I

will come back and see you again. José will take care
of me."

José had friends working in the mines. If he had
been alone it would have been a simple thing to find
a job and sleep with other miners in bunkhouses pro-
vided by the company. He found a place for his
mother at last in a miner's family, where she had a
room of her own and helped with the housekeeping,
and for the present she was settled and content.

Juliano had to get one of his grandsons to read the
note, which José had written, from Rosa. And when
he had heard it, he passed his hand across his eyes as
if to brush away a vapour. He took the letter from the
boy's hands and stared at it, turned it over and over
in the fingers of his one hand. What new madness was
this, come to assail an ageing man? Who ever heard of
a woman running off with her own son? And what
was the nature of the strange feeling around his heart?
He raised the letter again and studied the meaning-
less scrawling on the page.

Sending the boy away who had read the note, he
called to Nina who came running, as she always did,
to anyone's call.

"Look, Nina—what Rosa has done." And he
handed her the letter.

"What does it say?"

Juliano recited it from memory.

"Ah, then," said Nina. "I'm not surprised, really. We've been cruel to her."

"Cruel to her?" growled Juliano. "We've sheltered her, protected her when the people were ready to drag her away and give her a beating. She's an evil woman, Nina. And now she runs away—and takes my oldest son. That's bad for a man, Nina, for his oldest son to go away."

But Juliano's voice was quavering a little—enough to convince Nina that his hardness was mostly feigned.

"No," she said. "She's not bad. Not all bad. And you're sorry she's gone, Juliano. I can tell. She'd be glad to know that, but—I guess she never will."

Juliano, without looking up from the ground, mumbled in such a subdued tone that Nina missed it: "She says she'll be coming back some day."

"Well, now we'll see how we'll get along without Rosa," Nina said. "We'll miss her. Things won't go so well. You'll see."

CHAPTER VIII

Rosa tested and tasted her new life like a child with a new kind of candy. Their surroundings were if anything poorer than those she left, but she was used to that. The only money she ever saw now was what José brought to her, out of his wages, and most of that was not money at all, but something the miners called "scrip". It was good only at the store which the company owned, worthless in the larger stores at Antonito. Anything that the company store did not have, Rosa could not have. But this was all right, too. She had few needs and fewer material desires, and her happiness was not dependent on them.

The freedom of being welcome was bliss to her. To be regarded without fear or hatred was what she relished most. The people were different here, though. They seemed to have passed beyond belief in witches and to have settled in a more mature mode, like people grown from children.

Looking back on her little valley Rosa saw only children there, wearing the clothes of men and women. It was such a strange thing that she wondered why she had not seen it before, while she lived among them. Here men were occupied with machines about which there could be no romancing, and the women came under their shadow too. A man had to be grown up in this new place, for it was no child's business to dig underground and consort with engines which had the power to deal death to a man if hc wasn't careful with them. It made them sober, somehow, and pushed their lives into a groove and squeezed the fancy out of them.

This was not all good. Rosa liked a man with a song in him, pitied most of these miners whose lives were as drab as the black earth they worked in.

The dirt disturbed her, too. Over all things a powdery black dust settled. If you tried to pick a spear of grass to chew in this place as likely as not you'd get a mouthful of coal-dust with it, and it entered the houses and the food like a grim reminder of the master, coal. It was not long before Rosa hated coal, and the sombre shade of all things in that cruel cleft in the hills where she lived.

But she was free, and it was good. The houses were strung like a string of worn and shoddy beads along a black street at the base of a hill which was one side of the canyon where the mines were. Opposite, across a little stream which after a rain ran thick with black water, was another line of wooden shacks exactly like the rest. Because the mines used electric power, each

of these sorry houses was equipped with electricity—
a luxury as fantastic as green grass growing out of a
pile of evil-smelling, smoking, rust-red and black
mine slag.

Rosa felt these grotesque contrasts without enum-
erating them. They were a threat to her free and
joyous spirit. But when she felt the pressure of them
too much, she would walk alone down the black bed
of the stream until it was no longer black and she
came to a spot she had found one day, where a clear
spring stood in a little pool under the banks of the
creek, and sparkling water trickled away and green
grass grew and a few cottonwood trees. This was as
different from the coal-blasted slopes around the
camp as she could wish, and the knowledge of its
presence there was always a comfort to her. In Vallecito she had grown accustomed to clean air and the
fresh, unsoiled green of growing crops; this was a
fragment of hell compared to Vallecito.

But only in appearance. The man of the house
where she was living was about her age, perhaps
somewhat younger, and he had not been entirely
crushed by the mines. He had a guitar and he could
sing with a thin but true tenor voice. He reminded
Rosa a little of Ben Ortiz. His wife, impressed by
black work and child-bearing into a tiny, corruscating
point of vitality, was jealous of him. She was suspicious of Rosa from the day she entered the house, and

Rosa was careful not to arouse her too much, for she had seen her in a fury more than once. But the man was attractive, and an old game which she had almost forgotten enlivened Rosa's days. He responded to the gaiety she brought into the house, and they sang songs together.

José came to see his mother nearly every day, for he was working nearby on a night shift. He usually came in the late afternoon, after he had slept and before his work began, and she was glad always to see him clean and washed and not with the grime of the mines on him, like the men who passed the house all day. Often they walked down to her spring where the cottonwoods were, and sat on the cool, grassy bank while they talked.

"Are you glad you came away, mother?" he asked her nearly every time. "This isn't as nice as the valley —all the dirt and soot."

"Yes, José. I'm glad. It's dirty and poor, but—oh, the people are not children, and I feel so free. It's good."

"How do you get on with the family you live with? Are they nice to you? Do you like them?"

"Oh, yes. Onofre—that's the man—is very nice I think. He gets drunk every Saturday night, but he's a pretty good man. And Juana—that's his wife—she's jealous of him. I have to be careful. But I help her in lots of ways. I make clothes for the children, and do some other things. I think she likes me all right, but maybe she thinks I'm after her husband."

Here Rosa would always laugh, as if such a thought were quite absurd. And José would laugh with her.

"Their oldest boy works on the same shift with me now. He thinks you're wonderful."

And Rosa brightened. "Does he? I'm glad. I think he's a very nice boy."

Rosa preened in the silent glory of being told that she was wonderful again! Oh, yes, she was reborn in this black and grimy place. But she grew serious quickly and turned an anxious face to José. "How about you, José? Are you happy? How can you like such work? I see the men coming home, with coal in their hair and hands and faces—black ground into their skin. I never see you like that. I'm glad."

"I like the work. I don't know why. They say that a man grows to like the mines—once a miner, always a miner. It's true, I guess. There's nothing else I want to do."

She frowned. "I wish you didn't have to give me money, José. That worries me. I know it isn't very much, but—— Maybe you'd like to be married, and——"

He laughed gently. "No. I'm not in a hurry about that."

"Is there a girl, José?"

He looked down at his hands.

Rosa drew back with a sigh. "Ah, there is, then."

"No, there isn't really. I've just been thinking a little about one. I'll bring her down to see you some-day, if her mother will let her. She has three brothers, too, and they're all jealous of anybody who—who comes to see her."

"I'd like to meet her," Rosa said. "Maybe you could take me up to her house."

"Yes, maybe I could do that."

Rosa was puzzled for a time by his lack of enthusi-asm, and then it struck her that perhaps José was in some way ashamed. A woman who ran away from her husband and family—— "You've told them about me?" she asked thinly. "They know I'm here?"

"Yes, they know."

"What did you tell them, José? About the valley, and—and how the people called me a witch?"

"No, no, I didn't tell them all that!"

"What, then?"

"Well, I just told them that you felt unhappy there, and came away with me."

Rosa thought he was lying, but she didn't want to make him any unhappier by pressing him to tell the truth. "I hope you'll bring the girl down some day," she said.

"I will."

It was soon time for him to go back. They walked up the canyon in the twilight. The land didn't look

so black and forbidding. When the great gaunt
skeleton of the colliery came into view it looked
almost beautiful, with jewelled electric lights shining
like stars trapped in its labyrinth of beams. If she had
not been so saddened by her son's embarrassment of
her, Rosa might have sensed the beauty all about and
her heart might have dropped some of its heaviness.

But no, here was a new thing to worry about. She
must not always remain a burden upon José. She
must relieve him of that, somehow. She stood outside
in the dirty black road for a long time after José had
waved good-bye, and watched the lights blinking on
the colliery which climbed the hillside in giant steps,
and waved a flag from its topmost pinnacle. She could
see it up there, black against the dark blue sky. A
confused, low clatter came from the tipple, and
occasionally a sound like thunder as a load of coal
roared down the chutes.

She pressed her fingers to her temples. This incessant sound and work! Why must those wheels be
forever turning? Why must men go down into the
earth day and night? What was the good? Whom
did it serve? Not the men, surely. Not José or Onofre
or Juana or herself. Ruthless whining cables and
turning wheels! The word stuck in her mind—the idea
of ruthless. She didn't blame men for becoming so at
last, for not until they did were they completely the
masters of their world and their lives. These machines

were ruthless to them, the mines were ruthless, and the only defence against it was ruthlessness. She must learn that herself, and practice it.

She went inside. Little Juana gave her a sharp look out of her mousy eyes. Where had she been, with all the work to be done? And Rosa smiled. Women were too soft to live by themselves. Look at that Juana and the softness that lay at the core of her, underneath her tough little body and her ferocious manner. Herself, too. Soft, soft. Tender where tenderness should not be; hard where it did no good.

She did a few things to make Juana think she was helping, and soon slipped into her own room where she lived so much alone. Save for a few yellowing photographs, stiffly posed and grim, which she had stuck on the walls, the little room was lifeless. It was a cell. The ancient plaster showed patches of skeletal lath where it had fallen, and the colour of it was dirty grey.

She sat down on the bed, and closed her eyes against the dim and soulless room. Soon she began to talk, in a voice so low and yet so charged with erethic intensity that, though it sounded potent in her ears, did not carry beyond the door. Once or twice before she remembered doing this, soliloquizing in a lonely room like an actress practising her lines. It was as if she spoke to a ghostly audience who could see her facial changes as she played upon this string and that, and the gestures of her arms and body as she pointed her words.

At first her attitude was prayerful with an abject beseeching in her voice—"Oh, Mother of God. I am Rosa. I have done many wicked things." She opened her eyes and raised her face to the discoloured ceiling. "You see me now in my loneliness where my sins have brought me. Ah, sins!" She stood up, her supplication changed all at once to defiance. "They were not sins! I was innocent of any wrong. They were cruel, and it wasn't wrong to run away from them. And you, Juliano—you loved me once, long ago. But it wasn't enough! Oh, don't you see? You loved the land more than me. The land made you happy or sad. I had nothing to do with it." She swung around dramatically, as if to face an adversary. "That isn't enough! It may be enough for some of you women, but you are cows—cattle—sheep. It wasn't enough for me." Now she put her hands to her hips and sneered at an imaginary Juliano. "You thought you could keep me, didn't you, and feed me and beat me when you were displeased. Ha! I guess you know better now. I hope you're lonely, Juliano, lonely as I am sometimes. And I've got José, I've got your oldest son. He's my oldest son, not yours! He loves me. He's husband and son to me now!" She held her pose for a moment, then sagged at the middle and sat down again on the bed.

"Oh, José, I should let you go. I should let you go! A young man doesn't want an old woman on his hands. Marry your little girl, José. She's itching for you. She ought to be if she isn't because you're a fine, beautiful young man, José. You're good to me, so you'll be good to her—not like your father, sour and jealous and bad-tempered."

She jumped to her feet again in a swift change of mood, and she beat her breast theatrically. "I'll leave you alone, José. I'll do it. I'm not through yet. I can look after myself. But you'll never know—-I'll never tell you the reason. Not until I die, José—then I'll tell you, so you can remember me happily. So——" she spread out her arms pleadingly, "you'll hate me then for a while. I won't mind, José. I'm used to hate. I can stand hate. Didn't I live on it for years? Yes, marry your girl, José. Take her to bed. Give her what she wants. It's good. Nothing else is good in this dirty black hole. Only that. Only love."

She dropped into a chair and flung her head back. "Love. What is love? Too seldom pure. It gets all mixed up with other things and gets killed like a bird in a storm. Oh, pure, pure bird! White bird with a heart that bleeds if you look at it. I've had you here in my heart"—she laid her hand gently on her breast —"but you got away, each time. Each time you got away, white bird. Did I let you get away? Or did you go—ah, that's it. You have to be free. But I wanted you to be free. Wouldn't they let you?" Her eyes were burning in their sockets now and tears rolled from them. "What was it, white bird? Could you be white here, in this dirty place? Would the black soot settle in your wings and turn you into a crow, squawking over the black canyon? Can you live in such a place as this, white bird?

"Oh, I have killed you more than once! I've seen your blood redden your soft white breast. A woman's breast is soft, too—soft as yours, and it bleeds like yours, only the blood doesn't show. It goes back inside and comes out again like new blood, when she's hurt again." She jumped to her feet and clenched her fists. "But a woman can fly away, too! Yes, a woman can fly away and come down in a black canyon and still keep her heart open for the white bird, keep it pure through soot and sorrow to welcome the white bird. Ah, woman—the bride, always the bride. That's the woman's hour, when the white bird comes to sleep in her heart!"

And suddenly Rosa found herself with nothing more to say. Her eyes were dry, her breast stopped its heaving and her heart returned to its natural pace. She looked at herself in a mirror, frowned. Into a cracked basin, from a cracked pitcher, she poured some water that had coal-dust in it, and she bathed her face, dried it, tucked in some straggling strands

of hair. Then she went into the other room to help
Juana.

She was gay that night. No memory lingered of
what she had spoken to herself as another person—
she could not have told any of the things she had
said. While Juana sat sewing under a cone of light
after dinner, Rosa and Onofre sang songs to his
guitar. And when he stopped and stretched and said
he wanted to walk up to the store to get some tobacco,
he asked Rosa to come with him. Juana paid no
attention to them.

She let him touch her that night. The first time.
And she knew by his touch, by the steely resolution
under it, that his future lay in her hands. She went
to bed with a fluttering bird in her breast. She was
not too old, then! She could still inspire the touch of
a man. She sang good night to Juana so gaily that
that pinched and impounded woman smiled.

Rosa almost forgot that all this was for José. She
saw her designs fitting together so snugly that she felt
again like a goddess with a marvellous power in her.
The only difference was that Onofre was the leading
puppet now, with José in the wings. When Onofre
asked her to run away with him, she was ready.

By burying her in the mountainous obscurity of
bony hills and black coal camps, the world lost a
great actress in Rosa Trujillo.

CHAPTER IX

LATE in July the rain came to Vallecito. All through
the month, as if to torment the people, great storms
heaved over the mountains and sped out over the
plain. From a high place a man could see four or five
at a time, solid, dark grey masses sweeping slowly
across the sky with curving curtains of rain hanging
from them. And with what seemed like sensible design they avoided the valley and taunted it by ap-
proaching within half a mile of the parched fields.
The people gained one small victory over the per-
verse elements with their ditch, for rain in the mountains swelled the stream, and gave them water for
irrigation.

How they drowned their fields in it! Day after day,
first one field and then the next sucked in the water
and the men waded jubilantly in the mud, plastered
themselves in it from head to foot, wallowed in it like
swine.

But still no rain for the valley itself, and in between
storms above the stream dwindled to nothing, and
the people were plunged again and again into gloom.

When it came to the valley the rain came with a roar and a flood. They saw it coming. The whole world turned slate-grey and the day grew so dark that people came out of their houses to see what was wrong. They gathered in fearful groups to watch the piling black cloud-masses and to see the rolling ramparts of cloud obliterate the sky.

Oh, it was a frightening sight! Lightning flashes split the grey heavens like vast rips in a dark drapery which were instantly sewed up again while thunder echoed in the hills. Men left their fields and went down to inspect the banks of the stream, especially where they adjoined their cultivated land and feverishly strengthened the dikes with anything at hand. Juliano and his brothers and sons worked like ants at a turn in the bed of the creek where a flood might leap the banks and carry away a cornfield. Juliano directed the work himself, shouting and pointing with his one arm like an old war-torn general, or rushing into the thick of the work with an axe, slashing fiercely at the willows, felling them, while others dragged the branches away and jammed them into the bulwarks.

Before a drop of rain fell in the valley proper, the flood came down the stream. The men at the mouth of the canyon saw it first, and heard its roar of continuous thunder before they saw it, and gave the alarm in relays down the valley. They had closed the inlet of the ditch with a huge dike, and hoped they had saved that much anyway. It came crackling down the stream in a three-foot curling crest, tawny, sliding like a monstrous serpent. And in a moment the rain began, bursting from the sky like water from an opened flood-gate, solid, breath-taking. In no time the earth had turned to water, the ground underfoot was mud, and water poured from the hillsides and across the fields in brimming rivulets. The valley road, within five minutes, was a rushing torrent a foot deep while the volume of the flood increased. Men stood on the banks and watched the stream. Fear squeezed their hearts. Under the muddy waters they could hear the crash and rumble of rocks hurtling downstream in the clutches of the flood, and soon a whole cottonwood tree came down and lodged for a while in midstream opposite Juliano's dike. Water surged around it while floating sticks and litter caught in its branches and made a dam. Juliano yelled for poles. Frantically they struggled to dislodge the tree, and water licked the very tops of the bank, then came over the top and melted the dike away like sand. They had to run for their lives.

Oh, the roar and the fury of it! Water, water, ripping down the hillsides, tearing great caverns in the earth! Juliano watched, helpless, now, from the middle of the cornfield. The flood slashed across the lower end of it, leaping into the air like an exultant fiend, and water rose knee-deep in the field where he stood. Lightning blinded him and thunder smote his ears and the flood growled the undertone. He had a spade in his hand now, and he leaned on it. Oh, the land! The good land! God leave him some of it, turn back the waters from his land!

He turned and sloshed through the mud toward his house. What kind of a God was it, then? Was He an ironic God, who answered man's prayers for rain with flood and destruction? Why, why must such things be? Savagely he tried to stop a growing gulley in the field being formed by water rushing down from above, and his puny shovelfuls of mud were carried off as fast as he dropped them into the hole. He gave up, and moved on. Flinging his shovel down in the *placita* he went inside and found water there, too, coming through the roof in streams, soaking everything, pouring down the walls and carving channels in the mud plaster. Poor Nina had every available pot and receptacle on the floor to catch the water, but it was hopeless. It rained inside as well as out, and everything would go, nothing could stand against the onslaught.

It was over in half an hour. The black clouds passed, the sun came out and innocently looked down upon the slaughtered land. And people emerged from their houses and returned to their fields. Not all had suffered, but Juliano's cornfield was a ruin. Not a spear was standing, and the lower end, a half-acre at least, was simply missing, gone with the flood. He went out and stood on the brink of the cut the water had made, and he stared down into the angry river-bed, where naked rocks lay in ruinous abandon and a foot of muddy water still slipped noiselessly down. For a long time Juliano stood looking into the wreck of the stream. He noticed how like a drowned woman's head were the projections which had caught bits of grass and twigs and now, high out of water, stood with sodden tresses bent by the direction of the flood. He tramped over all his muddy fields, leaping across the gulches carved in them by the rushing waters, and he could have cried like a child to see the devastation there. Only the alfalfa, whose roots went deep, would gain by the flood, but one of those fields was half buried in gravel where the waters had swept across it.

Beatriz joined his brother, and Cruz, and some of the older boys, and together they moved in a slow tour of inspection across the Trujillo fields. Up and down the valley it was the same—men walking solemnly with troubled, frowning faces. Within the houses women were mopping the messes of mud and water wrought by earthen roofs which were never intended to withstand such a drenching. In three places Nina could see the sky through her roof; the earthen floor of the kitchen, usually hard as rock, was an ooze of slimy mud.

She was in tears when the men came home.

"It's nothing," Juliano said gruffly to her. "This will dry, and be the same again. But my fields! The corn and the grain and the beans. Gone! We've got to plant all over again in July. How can we get a crop? Half my cornfield—gone down the river. Somebody down by the Rio Grande has got it now. All that good soil! I always said it was better to live down there." And he added a strange, half-spoken thing: "I wish Rosa was here—she'd know what to do."

Nobody heard him. He hardly heard himself, so instinctive and unaware it was. And when he went outside again he shook his fist at the sky. "If I were God, I'd be God, and not a fool," he muttered. "Ah, Rosa——"

Slowly the men redeemed their fields. Up and down the river were ruin and destruction. The banks of the stream had to be reinforced. Cedar posts had to be cut, stone hauled. It was not often that the innocent-appearing stream showed its power, but often enough to keep men from forgetting it. And each time, it seemed, the power was greater, bound to destroy and tear down their best efforts to defend themselves. They had to rebuild parts of the ditch, for the waters had jumped the dike where the ditch took off and raced along the course, breaking carefully shovelled edges, ignoring its turns and windings.

In a man's mind the ditch was alive. It was something that needed looking after, like a cow or a burro

—yet less like a burro. Those little fellows carried their crosses on their backs and looked after themselves. They could find sustenance in the wilderness. Not so the ditch. Men owed a debt of vigilance to the ditch. It carried water in its arms, lifted it out of the indifferent stream and spread it on a man's fields. A man could do without anything except the ditch, he could do without love more easily. He could stand up against any loss, a wife or an arm or a friend, but the loss of water for his fields was a threat of death.

Every man whose land the ditch crossed—and no man in the valley escaped—felt a personal wound in the ravished banks and torn channel. And the ditch was his first concern; the fields could wait, the houses could wait, but the ditch must flow. The ditch must flow.

From the head of the valley above the farm of Ben Ortiz where the ditch began, down to the Sanchez place where Rosa met her doom was not a great distance, but in that space were a dozen farms and on each farm were breaks in the ditch. At the end of it some inventive Sanchez had rigged a pipe on stilts to carry the water out over the bank to keep it from cutting into their poor but precious land. Usually, however, the Sanchez family used the last drop of water that finally trickled the length of the valley down to their farm, and none was left to spill out of the crazy pipe into the dry river-bed, to sink at once into the sand.

That pipe was a ruin now, and a slow drip of mud fell from its middle joint, and the end of it pointed accusingly to the sky.

Two men from every farm set out, even before the end of the day of the flood, to mend that section of the ditch which crossed their lands. And where there were not two men, the women helped. They shovelled the silted course of the ditch, cleaned it of leaves and branches and rocks and built up its sides again and restored its turns. And by nightfall the ditch was intact again, and men could think about their fields.

The havoc there was not as great as they first supposed. Juliano and his brothers suffered most, for the flood had cut across the cornfield and taken it away. No changing that. It was gone. Other men's fields were covered with silt, but not so deeply that their crops were smothered. Within a few days shoots appeared above the silt and it was not long before the fields were waving lakes of green.

When Juliano, with his brothers, had finished new dikes along the stream, of interwoven, pliable cedar boughs and rocks held in place by posts and wire—he had leisure again for the education of his one remaining arm.

For he discovered afresh, through the emergency of the flood, how handicapped he was, how a one-

191

armed man was not much more than half as good as a whole man when there was quick work to be done. It angered him every time he thought of it; in his walks among the hills with his nephew's small rifle he lived again and again some of the intense moments of the flood. With two arms he might have dislodged that tree which caused the waters to overflow his dike; he might have been able to shovel quickly enough to stop some of those destructive channels that formed in the fields. Oh, he might have done many things that he didn't do. And with the rifle he practised shooting from his hip without aiming the gun with his eye at all. It was no good for a long time —he couldn't hit anything. From the shoulder he was getting better, though. He could hit the target about three out of five times.

Bland summer weather, with an occasional shower. Beatriz went in to the town with six burro-loads of wood to fetch some chickens for Nina and some ammunition for the little rifle that Juliano used. And he came back with the news that he had a hard time selling the wood in the town. The place, to one who visited it so rarely, seemed to change all at once instead of by a slow normal growth, and Beatriz was astonished to see so many streets, so many people, and the trees in the *plaza* and along the streets had grown until they shaded everything in a pleasant coolness.

It had taken him a whole day to peddle his burro-loads of wood where before it used to take an hour at the most. Why was this? Well, they told him that people used coal now which the railroad brought in from the mines to the south, and they didn't burn as much as before. And the old fort was gone, too—no more soldiers on the streets—and the houses where the soldiers lived all had coal stoves and were lived in by ordinary American people. These changes were not new, but they seemed new to Beatriz, and he was saddened by them. He didn't feel comfortable in the town any more—so many Americans everywhere, and the people seemed to be submerged and pushed into the background—his own people, the Mexican people who had been there so long before the Americans ever heard of the place.

Juliano said: "But that's nothing new, Beatriz. That's been going on for many years."

And Beatriz scratched his head. "Well, I never noticed it so much until this time. That new road, too, that comes north out of town—it isn't safe for burros any more. Automobiles go along so fast that you hardly have time to get out of their way. I almost got hit twice coming home."

"Well, we can always sell wood there in the winter. We can always fall back on that, you know. They've got to buy our wood. Because the Americans, they won't go out and cut it themselves, and the town's full of Americans. It's a good thing, too. We're going to have to cut a lot of wood this fall, because the crops won't be much good, with the dry spring, and that flood."

They talked about the changes in the great world while they sat in the *placita* looking along the valley which never changed. And Juliano wondered aloud sometimes about José and Rosa, if he had found work in Colorado, and how they were getting along. Never a word from either of them in all this time. At such times, after he had finished speaking about it, the memory never failed to return to him of the last words in Rosa's letter, some day I'll come back and see you again. And upon that peg, without his knowing it, he had hung his hopes and his future.

He would have denied it angrily. If Rosa's name was mentioned in his hearing he would growl and walk away. But in those secret thoughts of his, sitting silently in the *placita*, the truth was told.

In his spare time, Juliano fenced Rosa's old vegetable garden for Nina's chickens, and built an adobe chicken-house for them. But they didn't do so well. Nobody had anticipated the enemies of chickens— sickness, vermin, small animals, hawks. The first batch of chicks was a tremendous event in Nina's life. She cared for them like babies, but still they disappeared, one by one and no one knew why. Until one afternoon, just before the hens took themselves inside the toy house for the night, Nina spied a big bird wheeling, wheeling over the chicken-yard. She watched it and waited, thinking it was a crow. It looked black, silhouetted against the brilliant western sky. Lower and lower it wheeled, and when she saw what it was, a great hawk, she called for help. Nobody was there except Juliano—the one-armed Juliano. He would be no good.

He came running out of the house. "What's the matter, Nina?"

"Look—the hawk! Oh, Juliano, find Beatriz so he can shoot it. He's after my chickens, my little ones!"

Juliano gave a look, went into the house and came back with his father's old rifle.

"I can't find the little gun," he said, "but maybe I can——"

Raising the heavy gun to his shoulder, Juliano took careful aim at the almost stationary bird and pulled the trigger. The explosion which shook him from head to foot was followed instantly by an explosion of feathers in the air—and what remained of the hawk fluttered to the ground.

Juliano was grinning as he lowered the gun and looked lovingly at it. Mud from the leaky roof had splattered the barrel and the stock; holding it firmly between his knees he rubbed the mud away and polished the metal with the sleeve of his shirt.

"It needs cleaning," he said to Nina. "Have you got some rags?"

"Yes, Juliano. Bring it in the house."

For an hour Juliano cleaned his old gun inside and out and, slipping the last cartridge into the barrel, hung it over his bed where it belonged.

PART THREE

CHAPTER I

Sᴉxᴛᴇᴇɴ years dealt variously with the Trujillo family. To Rosa, living still in Colorado with her miner lover, the passing years brought first release and happiness, then a dull, interminable time of poverty and at last intimations of death. She dwelt now almost entirely in a world of fancy. For little else was left to her. The man with whom she ran away was a drunken fool; the real world was a mass of disillusion. She was ill, and her pain reared a prison round her, shutting out the world of which she already had too much. Out of the past came thoughts of home and native soil, and these were her only passions now. Oh, the long hours! Alone, neglected, empty. José came to see her once and sometimes twice in a year, and he alone could lift her out of her dreams; but he never had knowledge of Vallecito, and she ached for news from home.

Her imagining became more vivid. Old familiar scenes flashed before her memory with a clarity that was frightening. She could see the house, the *placita*, the children whom she yearned to see now with growth, manhood and womanhood upon them. And

Juliano, too, she saw, and even heard. Oh, how she wanted to know how things were in that little valley! How she longed to see again that angular pattern of green fields!

The conviction gained that the time for her to return to die was close at hand. Next time José should come, she would ask him to take her home. Poor José! He was ashamed of his mother at last. If he only knew——

"These last ten years," Juliano was saying to his oldest grandson, "until a year or so ago, were the best we ever saw in Vallecito. Everybody had money. Everybody had a car—almost everybody—and the people got rid of all their burros because they didn't need to haul wood any more. The Americans used to come up here and bring us money—hand it to us, pay us five, ten dollars at a time for the whisky we made here in the valley. They couldn't buy it then. They made a law in Washington that took whisky away from the people. They said it was a crazy law but—I wish we still had it."

"Why could they buy it here, then?" the boy asked, not unreasonably.

"Oh, they didn't bother us—we've always made a little whisky here—not enough to trouble with, though. But we sold it cheap, you know, and the people in the town used to come all the way out here to get it. We didn't even have to take it in there. And everybody had money—cash—all they needed, for everything. Now——" Juliano sighed and looked down the valley where the only visible change was a petrol pump in front of the store and an old battered sedan standing beside it.

"Oh, those were good times," Juliano said wistfully. "Your uncles were all here—except José—and we worked hard and made lots of money."

"Why did my uncles go away?"

"They had to go away. The burros were gone—we couldn't cut wood any more around here because the government bought all the land for the forest—the national forest, and they won't let us cut wood there. We have to go twenty miles for wood now. Before we could cut it anywhere. So there was nothing for the boys to do after they took away that law about whisky. They had to go away and look for work."

The boy was losing interest in his grandfather's tale of woe. Plans were forming in his mind for a way to pass the hot summer afternoon. "Give me a penny, grandfather."

Juliano looked down sadly upon the boy's upturned face. "What do you want a penny for, boy?"

"To buy a piece of gum at the store."

And Juliano shook his head. "I haven't got a penny, *chiquito*."

Oh, what was the good of trying to tell the young

about the world's misery? They'd find out about it soon enough. The boy was right to run off without listening to an old man's complaining. But Juliano sat quietly in the *placita* for a long time, and the lad's coming and going was only an interruption of his thoughts.

Yes, they'd all been fools to let their burros go. They should have known that those good times couldn't last forever. Now things were back where they used to be, but still with some difference. Even if they had the burros, they'd have to go so far for wood——

Nina came out of the house, and he looked at her. His accustomed eyes didn't mark the change in her, from a bright-eyed, round little bird of a woman to a bent, grey-haired figure who hobbled with the aid of a cane. She blinked at him, ten feet away. "Is that you, Juliano?"

Ah, the poor thing, Juliano thought, she seems to get blinder every day. Something must be the matter with her eyes. "Yes, Nina. Did you want something?"

"Get me some water from the well, will you?"

"Yes."

She hobbled back into the house.

Juliano rose with some difficulty himself—his joints were stiff and rheumatic, too—and went to the well. Expertly he flipped the bucket down and hauled it up, brimming. A one-armed man could learn to do

things if he had the mind to. And he poured the
water into a waiting pail and took it inside.

Signs of prosperity, already decaying, were in
there, also. For one thing, a sloping tin roof painted
red had replaced the old flat earthen one that leaked
so badly in the rains. But inside were new pieces of
furniture from mail-order stores in Denver and
Kansas City, already showing the marks of wear.
Coloured pictures on the walls, framed in vast gilt
frames, a new cook-stove. Pablo's old gun, covered
with dust, hung over the bed as before.

Juliano put the water down on the floor and went
out again. Yes, it was too much to expect those good
times to last forever. It was just as well, too. Those
were mad times—everybody went a little crazy and
thought he was in heaven. How they spent their
money! Always buying, buying, second-hand automobiles, new beds, new tables—everything had to be
new, all of a sudden, and made somewhere else. In
the old days people used to make their own furniture,
but no more. Oh, no, they had to come from the
town, or from farther away, and they had to be all
shiny and polished, like a new automobile.

Juliano shook his head. He had never liked it, he
remembered. He had never approved. The young
ones, with money always in their pockets—they were
the ones who did it. They were the ones who went
crazy. Oh, but some of the old people did, too. It's

no good blaming the young people. The old ones should have known better. And yet, what can a man do except take things as they come? How can he see around the turnings of the path ahead? What must be, must be. They had always got along, one way or another—maybe it wasn't such a bad thing now that they had to struggle again. It might teach the young people how their fathers and mothers had to work and fight and save in the old days.

Some things, though, would never be the same again. It would never be a day's journey in to the town—unless a man had six loaded burros. But there weren't more than six burros left in the whole valley. Ah, this was a dangerous thing! This troubled Juliano more than anything else, he thought. A burro may be slow and lazy and small, but he was easy to keep and he could carry a load when nothing else could. He remembered what the boys used to say about it. "Oh, what do we want with burros? We can carry more wood in the cars, and much quicker. We'll never use burros again."

Yes, but now where were all the cars? Broken down —finished. No petrol to run them, and no money to buy petrol. And no more burros. Nobody had seen that far ahead. Oh, no. Now what?

Juliano couldn't answer his own question, so he shrugged, and got up from his place on an old cottonwood stump, and walked to the edge of the ditch. It was always a comfort to look down into the ditch and see the good water flowing there. But it didn't flow as it once did, a foot deep and swiftly. No, the water was shallower in the ditch nowadays. Ben Ortiz used to warn about it long ago, but they laughed at him. Watching the water, Juliano could hardly see it move. Well, more people were using it, that was all. Once in ten days was all the use of the ditch each farm had now. Once in ten days.

He walked on slowly, thinking as he went, down the lane and up the valley road, pausing often to lean on the fence and inspect the fields. No change there. The alfalfa was getting spotty—they'd have to plough it under and re-seed it soon—and he tried to remember how old those roots were. At least twenty years. He remembered the last time they seeded it—José was a boy of fifteen or so. But they couldn't do it now, not right away. Seed cost money—and there wasn't even a penny, to buy his grandson a stick of gum. . . .

A car was coming up the road—Juliano stood aside to let it pass, without looking back.

"Hello, Juliano. Want to ride to town with me?"

It was the man who owned the store.

"I've got to go in for a little while—would you like the ride?"

Juliano hesitated. He still had a distrust of these automobiles. "Yes, if—if you won't go too fast."

"Oh, no. Get in. The road's pretty good now. No rain. We'll be back by four o'clock."

Juliano got in. He was nervous because the land seemed to speed past the window so fast, hills seemed insurmountable; but the little car snorted up and down with such assurance that he was soon at ease, and talking to his friend, who was, in fact, distantly related to him. They called each other *primo*.

"Well, *primo*, how are things with you?" said the driver.

"Not good. It's bad—everything's bad. And you?"

"Oh, fair, fair. Not as much money in the valley as there used to be, though."

"No. Not as much."

"Looks like a pretty good year for beans and chilli."

"So far," Juliano agreed unwillingly, "but it's only midsummer. There's two months to go yet."

The driver smiled. He was younger than Juliano— he was the oldest son of the man who had founded the store—and his outlook was not all black. "What makes you so sour, Juliano?"

"Sour? I'm not sour. I don't like the look of things much."

"Why not?"

"Well—I don't know." Juliano felt too tired to go over it all again; besides this man, full of hope, might not agree with him, anyway. "It's all right if you own a store with a post-office in it—money coming in all the time. It's the farmer who has to worry."

"Oh, you don't need much money. You raise everything."

Juliano stared at him. "Do we? I suppose we raise shoes in the fields, and clothes and hats and coffee-pots and sacks of flour." Juliano pointed at his own shoes, all torn and soleless. "That's all I've got left."

They laughed good-naturedly over his joke.

"Well, I'm still giving credit," said the storekeeper, "and I will as long as I can. To those I can trust."

Juliano nodded his acknowledgement of the compliment—just then they were climbing a hill and the motor was rattling the little sedan convulsively.

Watching the passing landscape from the window, Juliano saw how different it looked from a car. It had no details; it was only a procession of coral-coloured hills, dotted with *pinon* and juniper. And then, when they came out on a highroad whose surface was shiny black and smooth as glass, they went even faster.

"This the new road?" Juliano asked.

"Yes. Good, isn't it?"

"Maybe it is for one of these automobiles, but—it's no good for horses or burros."

The driver smiled and said nothing. When they had gone a few miles he asked again how Juliano liked it.

"I don't like it very much. Too straight."

"That's what you want—a straight road. Makes driving easier—safer, too."

Juliano shook his head. "People go too fast." He looked without approval at the black spear of road ahead, piercing the landscape ruthlessly, slashing through hills, leaping *arroyos* on concrete bridges. Not much like the old laborious plodding on the back of a burro. And Juliano thought nostalgically of the burro. Now that they were almost gone he realized that he was fond of the stubborn little beasts. They were friendly, with their big soulful eyes and floppy ears. And the Cross of Christ striped in black on their spines and withers. Oh, it was an omen there, all right. The Cross of Christ. But it was no good, telling this man about it. He would only laugh.

They were in the town before Juliano finished with his reflections about burros. And the first thing he saw on the *plaza* were great trenches in the streets with men working in them, only the tops of their heads visible.

"What are they doing, tearing up the streets? What's that for?"

"They're laying new pipes. They say they're bringing natural gas to the town."

"What's that—natural gas?"

"Why, it's—it's gas from the earth. They get it from wells, and pipe it in and burn it—use it for cooking and heating. Didn't you ever hear of natural gas?"

"Maybe," said Juliano uncertainly. "You mean they use it—they burn it instead of wood or coal?"

"Yes."

"That's bad," he said.

"Bad? Everybody here says it's a fine thing."

"Maybe. If everybody here uses this new stuff—who's going to buy our wood?"

"Oh." The storekeeper's smile disappeared. This old man wasn't such a fool after all. "I didn't think of that," he said. Then he brightened. "I don't think everybody will use it. There's a lot of Spanish people in the town, you know. They won't use the gas—it costs too much."

"No, but—they cut their own wood."

Juliano's gloom was too much for the storekeeper. "I'll be back in a few minutes," he said, and vanished.

Juliano was deeply distrustful of all that he saw in the town, and he was glad when they were back on the highroad on the way home. He hadn't even liked the people, when he got out of the car and sat for a while on a bench in the *plaza* under the trees. He didn't like the way the people looked at him—his own people, at that. Something hostile was in their eyes, something just a little contemptuous. No, he didn't like the place any more, and before they reached Vallecito again he resolved not to have anything more to do with the town. He wouldn't go there any more. It was different, changed. It was getting too big, anyway—a man couldn't feel right there any longer. You never saw a friend. Only strangers everywhere.

When he got home he thanked the storekeeper for the ride and walked slowly up the lane to his house, thinking about natural gas and wondering what kind of mysterious stuff it could be that was brought to town in a pipe and carried to houses in the same way. He couldn't make much of it. When he told Beatriz about it, they puzzled over it together and arrived nowhere. If only José were in Vallecito, he'd know all about it and could explain. But José was gone—nobody had even heard from him in five years.

Well, he was too old a man to keep up with the world now. It was time he took it easy and sat back to look on. He was entitled to it, wasn't he? Hadn't he worked hard all his life, and the last third of it with only one arm, too! Depression was another word they were using everywhere, especially now that the people couldn't sell their whisky any more and had no money in their pockets. But who could tell what a depression was? Nobody had ever succeeded in explaining it to him so he could understand it. It was a word, that was all. Just another of those English words that had no meaning, or lost its meaning in translation into Spanish. Juliano could see how it was something that might happen to a man—but to a nation—no, it didn't make any sense at all.

Hard times alternated with the good—anybody could understand that, and it used to depend on the rain and the water in the ditch. And the will of God.

Now other things seemed to enter into a man's destiny. And Juliano, alarmed, called his two brothers together one day to talk about them.

CHAPTER II

THE house wasn't crowded any more. In the old place were only Nina and Beatriz and Juliano and two of Nina's unmarried sons, Juliano's youngest son, married now, with two children. Nine people in five rooms. That wasn't bad. Cruz still had a big family down in his house. His oldest boy hadn't been able to find work after he married, so he had come to live with his father, and he kept on having children as if he owned the place. Cruz was in a bad fix, but he was proud and he never complained to anybody, and he went on singing with his friends on summer evenings. Nina worried about him and insisted that those children didn't have enough to eat. It was hard to tell just what the condition of Cruz was. When he came up to the big house to talk with his brothers, they could see that he was worried, and they could tell by his clothes that he was in bad shape, but that was all. He wouldn't say anything about himself.

The brothers had no trouble in finding the causes of their misfortunes—but the cures were not as easy. Many things they were able to mention that no man could have foreseen. The failing water—they agreed at last that it was a fact—the collapse of the liquor business, the extension of the national forest, that new fence the government had just put up, without a gate in it, cutting them off from the pasture lands to the west, with a new yellow sign on it in English which only a few people in the valley could read. But they found out what it said soon enough. Property of the United States Government—one hundred dollars fine for cutting it. A mythical sum.

Cruz, who had been too occupied with his own troubles to keep informed of these new ones, didn't know about the fence.

"But who put it up?" he said. "Why? We've always used that land down below for our burros. How can they stop us?"

"They say it's Indian land," Beatriz explained. "The government has been reclaiming Indian land and fencing it. That's the east boundary of the reservation."

Cruz sighed, and without anger, with only resignation, said: "Seems to me the Indians get everything. If an Indian wants an eighty-dollar wagon all he has to do is ask for it and it's given to him. If he wants a well they dig it for him, or a windmill or anything. If he gets sick they send him to the doctor or the hospital. Why don't we get some of that?"

"Is anybody sick down at your place, Cruz?"

Cruz ignored the question. "Why do they get so much money?" he insisted. "They don't work the way we do. There aren't as many of them."

Silence while they all considered the question.

"Maybe," Juliano risked at last, "it's because we vote, and they don't. The Indians can't vote, you know."

"Vote," said Cruz hopelessly. "I'd rather have an eighty-dollar wagon and a good team than a vote."

His older brothers looked at him askance. He must be desperate to talk like that. Why, a man wasn't a man unless he could vote. And from somewhere, out of the limbo of memory, came a phrase to Juliano's mind. "This is a free country. By our vote we can get what we want—what we need. That's why it's better to have the vote."

Words. Juliano himself had no faith in them. And Cruz looked his scorn, but held his tongue. He could almost laugh if he weren't so troubled. "Well", he said, "I don't know what it ever got us."

Silence again.

"Is anybody sick down at your house, Cruz?" Beatriz repeated the question.

"Oh——" Cruz avoided their inquiring glances. "The kids—they don't seem very good." And he changed the subject quickly. "Well, what are we going to do? Can you think of anything?"

"We've still got two burros," Beatriz offered.

"Yes, but they're so poor I don't think they could walk to town. They'd die on the way."

"Other people in the valley are much worse than we are. They got no land any more. All the farms are broken up. Most of the families have only an acre of ground, or less. Remember how our father told us not to divide the land? He was right about that."

They all nodded.

"But we don't get enough crops," Cruz said. "There isn't enough land for all of us as it is, all together."

"No, that's true. But it's better than the others."

And with this comforting thought the meeting broke up. Cruz went home first, leaving Beatriz and Juliano talking on under the cottonwoods in the *placita*.

"I think we'd better go down and see what's wrong with Cruz," Beatriz suggested. "He doesn't look very good. Something's wrong down there. Nina's been saying that those kids aren't getting enough to eat."

"Does he still get things at the store?"

"I don't know."

Juliano stood up and stretched. "I think we'd better feed those two burros, Beatriz. They don't get enough to eat on the hills. They're pretty poor."

"But we've got no feed."

"Well, we'll have to get some—somewhere. Next time we cut alfalfa we'll have to feed them up."

Beatriz shook his head. "There isn't enough. The horses need more feed than we've got."

Well, Juliano couldn't cope with the problem now —he was too sleepy—too old, anyway. He went into the house and went to sleep on his bed.

Things were much worse than anybody realized down at Cruz's house. As he walked home, Cruz was deep in a black despair. He hated to enter the house empty-handed, time after time, day after day. He hated to look into the faces of his family, especially the grandchildren. They were hungry. They were thin and their eyes were black and bright and round each time he came home, and they did something to his heart, and brought a choking feeling to his throat. On the way he stopped at the store.

"I'm sorry, Cruz—you owe me ninety dollars. I can't give you any more."

And Cruz walked out again—empty-handed. What could a man do? Only despair was in his heart, no anger, no rebellion. When he got home he looked into the sack of beans. Half empty. And that was the end. No more beans for two months. He'd have to do something. He'd have to go to the neighbours, to his brothers. His sons were helpless, too; they went to the town looking for work and found none. From the boys who had gone to the mines came warnings to stay in Vallecito, that the mines were not working, that no jobs could be found, so it was no good going away.

And the railroad was still laying off men, not hiring them. It looked hopeless, utterly hopeless to Cruz. They could starve, and nothing could be done about it. His wife's family had been able to help for a while, but all the men had finally lost their jobs and that help ended.

All that was left for a man to do was to vote.

At last the storekeeper had to close his store. He got word from Washington that his post-office wasn't doing enough business to keep the office open, and that was the end of that. The people, if they wanted their mail, would have to go all the way to town for it. And all the storekeeper had was his stock of goods. He was generous with it still, gave away as much as he dared, some of it to Cruz.

And the valley baked under the sun. The shady north sides of adobe walls were lined with men and boys, leaning against them or squatting on the ground —sometimes they pitched horse-shoes, most often they talked, talked. Turkeys darted in pursuit of grass-hoppers, and chickens scratched in the empty soil. An occasional burro stood, lean and drooping, in the small shade of a stunted *pinon* tree. All were lean and bony, like the face of the land itself. And they waited. Over the valley hung an air of waiting, motionless, inert; the men, lined up along the cool north walls, talked of everything except their need, and pretended that all was well. But there were no weddings, no

217

bailes—and it was a sombre crowd who gathered at the church on the Sundays when the priest came. Rumours flitted along the north adobe walls each day—the Trujillos's last horse died last night. Don Jaime Martinez lost his cow. Ben Ortiz had gone to the town to ask for help with the water. He wanted them to rebuild the ditch so they wouldn't lose so much water by seepage. Ben was still the *mayordomo* of the ditch, the man who had charge of it and portioned the water among the families in the valley. They had to pay him a small amount in return for keeping the ditch in repair. So he was all right.

But he came back empty-handed, too. They had no money for such work, but they sent an engineer out to look at the stream and the engineer said there wasn't enough water there anyway, and they should all move to some other place.

This was a great topic for discussion against the north adobe walls. Move to some other place. What other place? A man could only laugh at such nonsense. What other place would have them, when all the land where water flowed had been taken and settled two hundred years ago? How could people leave their homes, anyway? What should they do, just pack their belongings and start walking?

No, it was a joke, such nonsense.

When it was time to harvest the beans and the chilli and the corn, everybody was busy again for a while

—but each man looking over the field had to shake his head and admit that it wasn't enough. Only about half what it used to be. With boys coming home almost every day, boys who had gone away to work for wages, some of them with families of their own, how could they all live on half the former harvest? Too many people—too many people. Everywhere the complaint was heard.

It was the son of Ben Ortiz who first brought the news, the boy with the withered arm. He came back from the town one day in the late autumn with heartening news which spread swiftly up and down the valley. A man could go to a place called the County Welfare Bureau and if he could prove that he was penniless and starving, he could get food for nothing.

Overnight the people realized that they were all penniless and starving and on foot, on burros, in wagons and one big party in the storekeeper's sedan —all went into town the next day and descended on the County Welfare Bureau.

Juliano and Beatriz went late in the storekeeper's sedan. And outside the office they joined the long line and settled down to wait.

CHAPTER III

JULIANO and Beatriz, waiting in the long line outside
the office door, didn't get in that first day. Juliano
saw the great number of people—not all Mexican
people by any means—asking for help, and he felt
somewhat easier about being one of them, somewhat
less embarrassed. For it was the first time in his
memory that the people of Vallecito hadn't been able
to look after themselves. He saw how the valley people
marched into the welfare office with their heads held
high, but their eyes betraying their shame. Before the
place closed for the day he got near enough to the
door to hear some of the questions that were asked,
and he shuddered.

Yes, it was humiliation, all right. He was glad when
the door closed, and they said the others would have
to come back to-morrow, glad he wouldn't have to
face the inquisition of those bright young American
women, who asked a man all kinds of personal questions that he had never even asked himself. How brisk
they were. How they went after a man, as if he were a
horse for sale! It was good to get out into the air

again, and to see the sun still shining, to feel its warmth on his face and to know that whatever happened the sun would shine.

Two of the men who had ridden in the storekeeper's sedan had reached the desk, and on the way home to Vallecito they answered numberless questions about their experience. Both had been told that an investigator would have to come out and see their farms, check the stories they had told, before they would give them help. And the more Juliano heard, the happier he was to have escaped the thing. They still had a couple of strings of chilli in the house and some beans. Nina's chickens were not all gone yet, either—a few old hens still hungrily squawked and laid no eggs. And two sacks of beans remained.

No, they could hold out a little longer. From what the men said, a family had to be really reduced to nothing. If a man had any credit anywhere, if he had anything on his farm that could be eaten or turned into money, these had to go first, before those smart young women would give him help.

Two of them were in the valley next day. Juliano saw them down at Cruz's place and walked down there to hear them. They had Cruz, looking miserable and hopeless, between them, asking question after question. One of them spoke Spanish with such an accent that Juliano could hardly understand her, and the other wrote Cruz's answers in a notebook.

"How many people are dependent on you? How many children are there in your family? How old are you? How old is your wife? How old are the children? When was the last one born? Are you going to have any more right away?"

Juliano blushed under his dark skin to hear such questions, and on they came, a stream, a torrent.

"Is there nobody here or in town who could help you? Have you no relatives with jobs, who could give you groceries? How many burros have you? Horses? Cows? Chickens, cattle? How many acres in your farm? What about your brothers, can't they help? What about your wife's family in the town?"

Cruz was soon bewildered and answered all the questions wrong; and Juliano stepped forward to his aid, making himself known with a tip of his old *sombrero*. "I'm this man's brother," he said. "My name's Juliano Trujillo. I live up there in that house under the cottonwoods." He pointed up the valley, turning as he did so away from their too-eager faces. Oh, it was a shame on a man to be forced to this begging!

"Have you applied for relief?" the girl who spoke Spanish asked.

And Juliano turned about reluctantly and faced her.

"No."

"Then perhaps you could help your brother here."

Juliano flinched. "No," he said quickly. "I can't

help him. I've got nothing. I—I went in yesterday, too, but I—there were too many ahead of me."

"Oh, I see. Your brother tells me that you all work your farm together. That's a very good idea."

"Yes, but it isn't big enough. And the water is failing."

Scratch, scratch went the pencil on the notebook. The girl who was writing never even looked up. And Juliano suddenly felt sick, and was sorry he had interfered.

"Didn't you get a crop this year?"

"We got a few beans—almost gone now. You see, we have about four acres and so many people to feed, and——"

"Well, exactly how many people?"

"Well, there's nine up at my place, and Cruz——" Juliano paused to count laboriously on his fingers, "And Cruz has ten down here."

"Nineteen people." The pencil scratched.

"You both have sons who are away, working for wages?"

"Yes, but they haven't sent us anything for a year —more than a year, now."

"They're out of work?"

Juliano nodded. "They all want to come back now, and work on the farm—all but one, my oldest boy, José."

"Where is he?"

"I don't know," said Juliano so softly that they had to ask him to repeat it. "You see they can't come back here. We've got nothing——"

At last the young women went away. They could see them up the road talking to the storekeeper. Juliano and Cruz sat silently together on a little bench made of adobe which they had left at the base of the house wall when the place was built thirty years ago or more.

"I hope they give me something," Cruz said at last. "The kids are hungry."

Juliano felt his heart so heavy that he couldn't stay there and talk to Cruz. He walked home, and on the way stopped in at the store. The owner was smiling.

"I'm going to open up the store again," he said.

"Why?"

"Those girls came and said if I would they'd give me orders for the people in the valley to get food, and the government will pay me."

"Oh."

"Looks like the people would get some help," the man went on cheerily. "It's only right, too. It's time they did something for the people here."

Juliano went out without answering him.

This was a new way to look at it. He thought and thought about it as he trudged up the road. Why was it time they did something? Why was it right to give food away? Never before had it been right. A man always had to work for the food he ate and the clothes he wore.

No, Juliano didn't understand the storekeeper's attitude. People in the valley had been down before to nothing, but somebody always helped them. Now nobody could help. That was the only difference. It wasn't anybody's fault. Certainly nobody was to blame if the water failed, or if they fenced off their grazing land or if the people in the town didn't buy much wood any more. If they burned that gas stuff, and it was better than wood, whose fault was it? It was too bad, but——

You had to take the bad times with the good, and how could you always expect somebody else to look after you? Certainly the people were still willing to help each other if they could. The storekeeper himself had done more than anybody else, but he had to eat, too.

No, it was all too complicated for an old man with only one arm. Juliano went into his house and lay down on his bed, and in a dream he dreamed of Ben Ortiz. He saw him as he was long ago, a tall, straight man with a black moustache, and a winning way with him. He saw him surrounded by all the girls of the valley, and lording it over the crowd of them.

And Ben was coming into his own again, in spite of his queer wife and his son with a withered arm. The son had married and was living with his father; and it was said that his first two children were half-witted. But Ben was *mayordomo*, and he had a certain small authority in the valley because of it. He was still popular, but people took care not to trust him too far, and it was doubtful if people really liked him. Nobody could name a single great friend of Ben Ortiz, man or woman. He spoke to everybody in the valley, and he smiled a lot, but they didn't really like him. He even spoke to Juliano now when he met him on the road, or talking with a group along a south-facing adobe wall. These friendly meetings moved from north to south walls with the seasons—shade in summer, sun in winter—and a thoughtful man would dread to see how much idleness these numerous groups portended, for all their laughter and singing.

The older men talked about it, decrying the laziness of the young. Why didn't they do something, instead of standing around all day? Nothing to do? Ah, nonsense. A man could always find something to do—make something to do. He could go out and cut some wood, or make repairs inside the house, build a bench or a chair or a table.

No, it was hard for an old man to believe that there was nothing to do. To cut wood you had to go almost twenty miles over the hills now; to make a chair required nails, lumber, tools. And with no money to buy them, how could the young men get those things?

Had they really come so low that all a man could do was stand in the sun all day?

Juliano, for one, didn't believe it. He wasted much breath complaining about the valley boys—and the girls, too. Why didn't they weave and work and make clothes as they used to do when he was a boy? No answer satisfied him.

And he was beginning to think he might get through the bad times without asking for help from those young women, when José and Rosa appeared.

They came unannounced one day, drove up the lane and stopped by the house. Nobody saw them until they had unloaded their few bundles and stood there together like a couple of strangers.

Nina heard the sounds of the wagon and looked out of the window, but her old eyes were no good and revealed only a blur which seemed of no consequence. Juliano was the one who found them, after the wagon, which brought them, had driven away. With Rosa leaning on his arm, José walked to the *placita* gate and stood there looking in. And he was still standing there when Juliano looked up from his seat on the old cottonwood stump, and felt his heart give a laboured leap and feebly go to work again. He wasn't sure—his own eyes were not faithful any more at such a distance—and he rose slowly and walked over to the gate, squinting at the pair standing there. And when he was sure he broke into a senile run, fumbled with the latch of the gate and took Rosa in his arm. It had been for a moment in his mind to spurn her, but his heart rebelled. Tears ran down his cheeks as he patted her back with his hand, with his face turned searchingly upon José, who smiled faintly at a cost of effort.

For it was not the same Rosa who had gone away. She was a wisp, a feather; her cheeks were sunken and her bony hands clutched at Juliano's sleeves, clung to the empty one like the claw of a bird. Juliano stepped back to look at her. And he spoke to her for the first time.

"Rosa—you come back again, no? But you don't look the same. You're thin, thin, Rosa. Are you sick?"

She nodded. And with a melancholy, far look in her eyes she said: "José brought me home to die. I asked him to."

"To die?" Juliano repeated aghast. And they walked into the *placita* together, Juliano slowly, faintly shaking his head. She was leaning on Juliano's arm now, and José came along behind them, carrying the bundles. Juliano seemed lost in a numb dispersal of feeling. They had advanced to the house door before he roused himself and called for Nina.

"Nina, Nina, look who's come home again! Come out, Nina, come out and see!" And with that, Juliano turned and embraced his son, as if he noticed him for the first time.

Nina, appearing at the door, peered out with her dim eyes. "Who is it? What do you yell for, Juliano?"

"It's Rosa, Nina! Rosa and José!"

And Nina burst out of the door and enfolded the frail Rosa in her arms. She could see her now vaguely, but she could feel better with her arms how she looked. "Ah, Rosa, you're thin. What's happened to you?"

José stepped up and to save his mother the pain of answering the question, said: "You'd better go inside now, mother. I'll bring your things in."

Nina, with an arm still around her, went into the house with Rosa, leaving José with his father. They looked at each other, and Juliano's eyes were full of a sad inquiry. José motioned him with a nod of his head to a place where they could both sit down.

"Tell me, José—tell me about her. Where has she been? What is wrong with her now that she looks so bad?"

"I went to see her," José began, "a few days ago— and I found her alone, sick—that man ran away and left her."

"What man?"

José stared. "You don't know?"

Juliano shook his head. "No. I don't know anything about her—not since the day she went away."

Briefly José told his father what he knew about

Rosa, and how, on the way home, he had discovered that she had gone with the miner because she wanted him, José, to be free of her, free to go his own way, marry, have a family and all the rest. She never told him, until now. And he, the fool, had never suspected the truth, had thought it was old wantonness, come to life again, and he had been ashamed.

Remorse was still heavy on his heart. That was why it was so hard for him to smile. And now she was going to die. Oh, yes, there was no doubt of it. She wanted to come home to die.

Juliano was grave. "Things are very bad here," he said. "It isn't a—a very good time for her to come. We're all very poor in the valley now. Everybody. You see—things have happened——" And in his turn he told José of the shadow that lay over Vallecito.

"We still have a little left here at this house—but Cruz——" Juliano shook his head dismally. "Cruz is in bad shape. He's got nothing left. Nothing. He had to ask help from—from charity."

It was not hard for José to catch the humiliation in that. The sag of his father's face, the droop of his shoulders, the hopeless hang of his hand by his side— all spoke of shame and humiliation. For charity was a thing for the shiftless, the inadequate, not for strong men and women who stood on their own feet. The Sanchez family, for instance, had always accepted charity, but the Trujillos—never!

Juliano was bewildered by the uncontrollable things which had befallen, and José could make little sense of what he said. To make it easier he decided not to stay after his mother died, which could be nothing but soon. Her death was written, somehow; he felt it, she felt it. Soon they would all feel it, as surely as animals do, after she had been in the house a while.

Rosa took to her bed at once. It was a bother, making necessary a rearrangement of the family, and now with Rosa down, Juliano wouldn't sleep in the same bed with her. And they had to find a place for him to sleep, and it ended by José and his father sleeping together in one of the white iron double beds with which the house was filled. So many of the young people were living in the town that they left a vacancy—until they, too, should come humbly home again, hopeless and out of work.

José was the one who cared for his mother. He sat with her for a part of every day, for the others had already come to accept her presence there, and even her impending death, as a matter of course, with even, José felt, a little impatience. And he couldn't forget the sacrifice she had made for him. Never, never would he forget that. He thought of his family up in Colorado, and how they would be needing him soon; of his job in the mine and how he might lose it if he didn't get back to claim it. But none of these things was strong enough to make him leave his mother, as long as her frail life quivered in that little room.

But she lived and lived, and at last José had to go. He made them promise to let him know when she died, and to take care of her while she lived. At least it would be better here than where she had been, alone in a miner's shack in the mountains.

A month passed. Juliano saw with sharp disdain the number of people who were going to the town and getting help from those young women. He saw how Ben Ortiz was getting it, when he didn't really need it, and how his son was using the money to buy his wife a radio. He complained bitterly about it, and he almost had another fight with Ben over it one day, when he brought up the matter with him.

He was a sly one, that Ben Ortiz. The other people got only food or clothes, but Ben got money out of it somehow. But not enough to share with anybody else. They weren't supposed to share it, anyway. If another family needed help they were supposed to go in and get it, and not borrow it from others. Juliano hadn't been in again, and he watched the supplies in the house dwindling, knowing in his heart that he would have to come to it sooner or later, and dreading the day.

Meanwhile, the harvest was gathered by the younger men, and the share for the three families was small. Juliano and Nina, drawn close now in the companionship of old age, talked freely about their plight and their needs, and in Rosa's hearing, too. She heard them say one day that of course the biggest share would have to go to Cruz because his children needed it most, and his house was full of grandchildren as well. And here the best would have to be saved for Rosa because she was sick and dying.

Rosa heard them talking frequently and she never heard anything but worried complaining because the strain of want was always present. And as little remained of her will to live, and a sense of guilt, now that she was about to die, hung heavily upon her heart, she came slowly to a determination which might, among other things, be good for her immortal soul. She would stop eating. She ate little enough, anyway, and the change from little to nothing would hardly be noticed. And before they knew it she would be dead and out of the way.

This decision illumined the tiny world in which she now lived like an ecstatic vision. No need to tell anyone about it; she was left alone most of the time. It was an affair between herself and her soul, which now appeared to be the most important part left to her, the one thing that was not doomed to die. And her soul became real to her at last. Before it had been only an idea; now it was something in her almost as palpable as a child in her womb. She could feel it

233

throbbing in place of her heart, waiting, eager for release; its destiny became her chief, her only concern. She had certainly jeopardized its fate by her sins—perhaps this last sacrifice would be some small atonement. . . .

No one knew the loneliness or the pain of Rosa's last hours. She died alone.

It was impossible to get José down from Colorado in time for the burial. They put her out in her best dress with candles at her head and feet, and darkened the room. Then they told the neighbours, who came all through the day to pay their respects to the dead. But the crowd was small. Many people had not forgotten her past. Juliano stole a moment alone in the room with her. Nobody suspected the tears he shed. Nobody saw in the calm, set face which emerged from the room at last, the grief of remembering which had broken him in there, secretly, darkly, with only his Rosa to know. Witch or not, who could say? In her youth and beauty was her witchery—that was her time for casting spells.

Few people came to the wake in the night, but Ben Ortiz was one who did, waiting on the edge of the small crowd until Juliano was away from the house. Then he went inside and stood for a moment beside the bier, his face a deep-creased picture of grief in the light of candles. Then he went away again and took his memories with him. Even now he didn't know whether he loved or hated her, but he was sorry for some things he had done.

"Too bad," they all said. Perhaps if matters had been less desperate with them, more tears and wailing would have sped her soul away. But as it was, a person could not simulate a grief which was drowned in relief. The men wore long faces and the women seemed ever on the point of crying—but no tears came.

"Rosa was a woman of character, all right," was a thought which spoke from many eyes, "but most of it was bad."

When José came a couple of days after the burial of Rosa, his father tried to make him stay—they could make room for his family, which was still small. "You're my oldest son, José. I need you here."

"No. The others are enough. They'll look after the farm. We're too many, anyway—the land here can't take care of us all. I don't want the land. I'm afraid I'm a bad farmer."

"You weren't a bad farmer before you went away, José."

"Maybe not. Maybe I just didn't know how bad I was."

"Will you go back to the mines?"

José nodded.

"It isn't good work for a man, digging under the ground."

235

"I don't mind it. You'll have a poor crop this year, unless you get a lot of rain in the summer. I'd better hold on to my job, and maybe I can help you next winter, with money."

Juliano could not deny the logic of it, but it was an added sorrow to lose José, after having already lost so much. He drummed the table by his side and regarded his shoes for a long time without raising his eyes. José sat astride a chair with his arms on the back of it. He, too, felt the sadness of this parting which he knew would be the last.

"You see," he tried to explain, "I—we learned what it was like to have money, and—and nobody ever has money here. It's only the land. Not enough land, for everybody."

Juliano raised his eyes. "My father told me when he died—you were a small boy then, José—never to divide the land we have here—always to work it together and share equally in it. If my boys go away, who will work the land?"

"But the other boys will stay," José said. "They're all good farmers. Good boys, too. They'll take care of you."

Juliano shook his head. "None of the young ones are good farmers any more. They're too impatient. Like you—they want money, not beans." He sighed. "How long will you stay away, José?"

José flinched at the question; an impulse to shout

rose to his throat. Forever! I never want to see this valley again, or any of the people in it! He bit his lip, remembering the number of times he had said those things to himself in the past. Didn't he hate this mean little place which drove his mother to homeless wandering? Didn't he despise the people who speeded her death? Yes! Yes!

But this man was his father, and he was old and tired.

"I don't know," he said.

"Well, maybe you'll come back some day, José. When you do, the land is yours. Remember that. You go against my wish. If some have to leave the valley it should be the younger boys, not the oldest. It looks bad."

"I'm sorry, father——"

"Oh, no. It's that war. I know. You were never the same after you came back. I didn't know you. You were like a stranger in the valley. Maybe you saw things, no? Maybe you saw things that changed you more than we could see?"

"Maybe," said José, staring at the floor.

And after a pause, his father said: "You loved your mother, José."

The son started in his chair and raised flaming eyes to his father, who quelled him with an upraised hand.

"I know. I loved her, too."

"You!"

237

Plain, the accumulated accusation in the word!

"Yes, me!" Juliano cried, but instantly his voice was soft again. "Some things, José—even if you did go to the war—you still don't understand. Only remember, when you think of me—I loved your mother, too."

José's retort was stilled. Before he could speak, his father left the room, went outside to sit in the cold moonlight in the *placita*. José went to bed; from a window he could see his father sitting there on the cottonwood stump, his shoulder drooping, his head low on his chest.

Some things age alone can feel. José left next day without properly knowing the pain his going caused. And Juliano, like an old tree, raised his head to storms yet to come, and his hair was grey.

After José's departure, Juliano sank to the pit of gloom. If any of them lived through this winter it would be a miracle. Terror was abroad, death was in the valley pointing a finger at them all. It grew cold and people shivered before stoves too meanly supplied with wood. Animals died. People died. Money was scarcer even than food. Juliano hadn't seen a coin for months. The end was near.

At last in desperation he called Nina and Beatriz to him and talked of what to do. Something had to be done. No money, almost no food. In a last defiant gesture, the two old men decided to make one more attempt to cut wood and sell it in the town.

They went out with two burros and worked all day in the high foothills, far from Vallecito, and it was night when they got home. Beatriz was tired and went to bed. And in the morning he was sick. He had a terrible cough and a fever and a pain in his chest. They got *Dona* Maria down to look at him, but she wouldn't do much because she knew they had no money to pay her. She gave him something to drink, and went away again.

Beatriz had been careful, he thought. He had wrapped some old sacks around his shoes which were full of holes, but they must have got cold and wet none the less. Well, he'd stay in bed for a few days— then they could go in and sell the wood. With three young men in the house, Juliano complained, it was a shameful thing that two old men like himself and Beatriz had to go out in the middle of winter and cut wood. But the young ones were in the town at the time, looking for work, and the food supply was low. They couldn't wait for the boys to come home. Nobody knew how hard they looked for work in there; they always came back looking hungry and beaten.

Juliano waited for Beatriz to get better—only a couple of days' supply of food remained. But instead of getting better in the next two days, Beatriz got worse. And early on the third day he died.

This was a terrible thing, taking everybody by surprise. Oh, he had seemed pretty sick on Friday night, but not as sick as all that. Now what could they do? Two deaths in one winter. They couldn't even bury him decently. The food was all gone, the children were crying, Nina was beside herself, with tears streaming from her red eyes. The boys were still in town, and Juliano was left with the whole difficult situation on his hands, alone. There was Cruz—he went down to tell Cruz about it, and Cruz agreed to stay at the house while Juliano drove one of the burros to town with a load of wood—which would bring fifty cents—and rode the other one.

It was a grey day, a Saturday. He didn't get started, with so many things to do before leaving, until mid-morning. And the sky was threatening. It might snow. Juliano put on his old sheepskin coat, ragged and falling apart in its seams, straddled the stoutest of the two burros, and started.

Now in the slow progress of the little beasts, whose bones showed through their shaggy coats, was time to consider the death of Beatriz. Before he left, Juliano and Cruz had put clothes on him and laid him out as nicely as they could on a table and covered him with a sheet. Nina put some candles around and darkened the room. But Juliano's principal thought had been, what an inconvenient time for Beatriz to die. By now, he thought, the news would be about and people would be coming in to help, though there was nothing much to do except comfort Nina and sit for a while in the closed room.

He watched the other burro anxiously. He was poor, and lazy. He wouldn't move faster than a slow walk, even down the hills, and on the ascents he stopped often. Juliano had to beat him on the rump with a stick to make him go at all uphill. The road was a procession of hills, up and down gaunt ridges of pink, crumbling rock, carved in naked, queer shapes by the rains. On bright days he had amused himself many times by noticing the animated forms of the shadows, but to-day there were no shadows, no sunlight. And it was cold; a bitter wind howled among the sandhills; charging gustily down from the north and twisting among the pinnacles and shapes, it attacked Juliano and his burros from all directions. The loaded burro, the one that carried the wood, seemed to move more and more slowly, and his nose all but scraped the ground. And Juliano, wrapped in his sheepskin, sank into a reverie in which he lived again all the scenes of his youth with Beatriz. Strange, he thought, that Beatriz should be the one to go first. He had never been sick in his life. People remained who still had need of him, too; Nina and his children. Oh, it was a strange world—a man couldn't know much about it. The best he could do was to take it as it came, accept it without crying or complaint.

Something always happened to help people over the worst of it, and for the rest it wasn't bad.

After a timeless plodding in the silences of the hills, lulled to dreaming by the flutter of burro-hooves, Juliano saw in the distance the straight line of the highroad, and automobiles moving along it like birds flying. He came out of his reverie and looked at his burros; the loaded one had fallen behind, far behind —he could see him as a speck on the tawny landscape, standing motionless as the rocks. He got off his burro and started back, brandishing his stick and shouting—and as if he saw what was coming, the loaded burro lay down in the road and leaned on his load of wood. When Juliano came up the eyes were closed and the lean ribs seemed not to lift at all with breathing. Juliano stared down at the beast. "Get up, you burro! Get up, get up!"

He pounded the grey flank with his stick, and the burro grunted faintly. It was no use—he'd have to take off the wood. Slipping the knot in the rope which bound the load, Juliano spilled the wood over the road. "Now will you get up?" he yelled, and beat the burro again. But instead of getting to his feet, the burro relaxed on his side with a great sigh, and stretched out his legs.

Juliano cursed and raved at him, pounded him with his stick.

Powerless with exasperation, he gave up and

stared at the prone burro. It was too much. He clenched his fist and raised his arm to the glowering sky. "*O, por Dios*, why must this happen to me now? Make him get up, make him take my wood to town!"

No answer came from the sky, but a gust of wind blew his hat off. He got down on his knees beside the burro as if to plead with him—and he saw that the little animal was dead.

In despair Juliano squatted beside his dead burro. He ran his fingers through the coarse coat, and patted it gently. *Pobrecito. Pobrecito.* He could be tender now that it was dead.

At last he got up, leaving the beast and his load where they lay in the road, and went back to the other burro which was trying to find a mouthful of grass on the frozen ground. He thought of loading the wood on to the remaining beast, but decided against it. He was too old to walk all the way into the town—and he'd need the burro to carry him. But he walked for a while, turning into the highroad and walking along the earthen shoulder of the pavement. Automobiles flashed by, so close that they raised the hair on the burro's back, but Juliano plodded on oblivious to all but the heaviness of his heart. Life had reached its darkest point, then.

It had begun to snow, and the cold was creeping through the cracks in his sheepskin coat. His feet were numb, for his shoes were hardly shoes at all any more. He had filled the holes with layers of paper before he left, but walking had quickly worn them through again. And how could he know that this second burro wouldn't die? He was almost as poor as the other one.

A premature dusk lay over the town when he topped the last ridge and looked down into the hollow where the city was. Still the cars passed, one every few minutes. Juliano never thought how many people saw, with differing emotions, an old, one-armed man astride the walking skeleton of a burro. No, he only thought of getting to town, and what he would do when he got there.

Only one thing occurred to him, now that he had no wood to sell. The Welfare Bureau. Maybe one of those young women would still be there. They could help him. If not—his mind was a blank beyond that. He could think of nothing else to do, with no money in his pockets and no wood to sell. He'd have to turn around and come home, he supposed. This burro probably couldn't last all the way. Well, a man could only try.

He left his burro in the street outside the office—it was much too tired to move, but he tied his sheepskin coat over its head as a precaution—and went inside. A light was burning in there, glowing through the frosted glass in the door. He breathed a prayer of thankfulness. But the door was locked. He knocked gently, and waited, listening.

Somebody was moving about inside. Presently the door opened and a young woman stood before him. She was pretty, Juliano thought as he glanced at her face, and she had nice brown eyes.

"What do you want?" she said in Spanish, and Juliano's heart warmed.

"Well, I—I came in to see if you could help me ——"

"We can't do anything now," she said. "The office is closed until Monday morning." She started to shut the door, but hesitated, seeing the dejection of Juliano's face, the state of his shoes and his clothes. "What is it? Is it something you need right away?"

Juliano tried to smile. "Well, you see—my brother, he died this morning, and—and we haven't any money or any food. And my wife, she died not long ago."

"Where do you come from?"

"From Vallecito—you know?"

"How did you come?"

"I came with my two burros, but one of them died on the way. I had a load of wood to sell, but—he died."

The girl sighed and shook her head sadly. "Well, come on in—sit down there while I close up." Then she muttered something in English. "I'm too damn soft-hearted for this job."

She arranged some papers on a desk, opened and slammed drawers. Juliano didn't know whether she was angry or only in a hurry. He watched her anxiously. How good it felt to be in a warm place!

She came over and stood in front of him again. "I can't possibly get you anything until Monday," she said. "Can you come back then?"

"Well, I don't know——" Juliano stood up slowly and looked down at the floor. "If you can't do anything, I guess I—I'll have to go back. I don't know what to do." He started to go out.

"Oh, wait a minute," the girl said, stopping him. "Where's your other burro?"

"Outside in the street."

"Wait—I'll go out with you."

When she had turned out the light and put on her coat they went out together.

"You mean to tell me you came all the way from Vallecito on that thing?"

Juliano nodded. "I walked part of the time, too."

The girl studied the burro, felt of his bones. And she spoke in English: "I can't stand that. If you're going back on that burro he's got to have something to eat." She opened her purse. "Is that the best pair of shoes you've got?"

"Yes—it's all I've got."

246

"What's your name?"

Juliano told her.

"And you're from Vallecito. I thought everybody out there was on relief."

Juliano shrugged. "I guess almost everybody is, but—we had a few more beans——"

The girl hesitated. "Why didn't you come yesterday—or this morning? I can't do anything now."

Juliano shrugged again. "Well, my brother, he only died this morning—and I didn't know. I came as soon as I could."

"Oh, come along. I'll tell you what I'll do. If you promise me you'll buy feed for that burro, I'll give you two dollars. Then you can stay in town to-night and go back in the morning. Do you know anybody here?"

"Oh, yes—I'll find a place. I've got some relatives here."

"All right. But you come with me first—I'm going to see that you feed that burro."

After they had been to a feed store, bought grain and hay for the burro, the girl left him. "I'll be out Monday morning," she said, "and see what I can do."

Juliano thanked her, and went up to the house where the family of Cruz's wife lived. They were not particularly glad to see him.

CHAPTER IV

THE young woman came on Monday. Beatriz was still laid out on the table, and she made haste to furnish money for his burial. He had been there too long.

And for the nine people in Juliano's house she was able to promise a total of 17.80 dollars a month, out of which sum they would have to furnish the nine with flour, cereals, potatoes, lard, sugar, baking powder, salt, soap and kerosene—if anything was left they could buy shoes and clothing with it.

She told them they could have a doctor, too, free of charge if they needed him, and Juliano, remembering what it had cost to have his arm cut off—a debt which was still far from paid—thought this was a great thing, if people ever wanted a doctor. For himself, he didn't like doctors. Most of them were Protestants, and you didn't want a Protestant in the house if you could help it. And he couldn't see that they accomplished much more than old *Dona* Maria, or a candle burning before a saint.

But the desperation of complete nothingness was

lifted from the house; at least from now on they could eat, and the children could go back to school. The young woman came out frequently to see how they were getting along, and they all grew fond of her. She had a heart, and she spoke good Spanish that people could understand, and she treated them with courtesy, not like beggars. She tried to persuade Nina to see the doctor about her eyes, but Nina said she was too old to bother with them—it was rather restful to live in a dimness after so many years of seeing life too sharply.

Juliano saved nickels and pennies in an old cow-hide box, and when, months later, he had two dollars and gave them to the young woman in payment of the loan she had made to him on that terrible day in winter when life had seemed down to the darkest depth, he was surprised and puzzled to see tears come into her eyes.

"No," she said, "you keep them." And she touched his bony hand that proffered the box and turned away from him quickly.

Spring came late to Vallecito, but the ground was good for planting, moist and fragrant from the snows. Although every man knew well that it would be a long, slow climb out of the well into which Vallecito had fallen, hope was fresh in their hearts. Water flowed in the ditch, and the men who worked on it under the direction of Ben Ortiz were happier than they had been for years. They had seeds, too, new, good seeds supplied by the young women from the office in town. Juliano was ashamed to hear how some of the people talked and complained about being allowed so little, when they needed so much. He was thankful for what had been given already, and looked forward to the day when they wouldn't need to ask for more. He heard that Ben Ortiz was one who complained—they had cut him off when they heard that he had a source of income from being the *mayordomo* of the ditch, but his son still took money from them.

And Juliano, seeing how Cruz barely managed to keep his family well and fed on the supplies he got, resented all the more the complaining of Ben and his son. He made up his mind to do something about it, and one afternoon he walked up the valley with the intention of investigating the old rumour about the radio.

And on the way he had to pass several adobe walls where men and boys were idling, some in the shade, some in the sun, for summer had not quite asserted itself. He paused at each place and made known his errand, trying the temper of the people. He found some who agreed with him, some who were indifferent, none who opposed him. Ben Ortiz, most of them felt, was endangering all of them by his cheating. The young women might grow suspicious, if they found out about Ben, and think everybody was trying to cheat. And they might cut off the valley again and leave it helpless, as it was before. Not many, however, cared to interfere, having troubles enough of their own.

But he picked up three recruits at various places who agreed to go with him to see Ben Ortiz. Juliano didn't want to go alone because he wanted Ben to see that other people were aroused as well, and it wasn't only the old enmity between them.

Ben Ortiz, they found as they walked four abreast up the valley road, had always been a little off. Nobody trusted him very far, though he was a likeable man in some respects. Now if he was really getting help when he didn't need it—if he was cheating those young women from the Welfare Office—it was up to the other people in the valley to do something about it.

When they reached Ben's house, therefore, the four men were in the heat of their righteousness, and clothed in their mission like men in dark cloaks. Ben was sitting by the door of his house talking to the storekeeper, and the four visitors squatted unobtrusively to join their talk.

"That's the only hope of the country people," the storekeeper was saying. "The land's worn out— they'll never make a living from farming again."

"They used to do it in the old days," said Ben,

nodding his head wisely. "They'll have to do it again —only now to sell their stuff, not to use it."

"That's right. Your boy sells his carving in the town, doesn't he?"

"Yes, he's been doing pretty good. He makes chairs and tables and seats and things, you know? He uses these green willow branches——" Ben was puffed with pride as he talked for Juliano's benefit, remembering an old quarrel about a boy with a withered arm. "He's done pretty good with it, all right. He gets two dollars for the chairs and three for a table or the bigger pieces. It only takes him a day to make them. He made twenty-five dollars last week."

"He still gets money from the relief?" one of Juliano's delegation put in suddenly.

This stopped Ben Ortiz in a hurry. He looked embarrassed for a moment, then smiled his most ingratiating smile. "Well, it's only lately he's been doing this. Maybe it won't last, you see. It isn't much money, anyway—a dog couldn't live on it."

All four visitors flinched at this, for all of them were living on it. "What does he do with all the money?" said Juliano.

Ben gave him a hostile look, started to make a hot reply, and thought better of it. "Why, he buys food for his kids, like anybody else would do. He helps his old father, too."

"Does he buy things he doesn't need?" said one of the visitors, looking hard at Ben. "Does he buy a radio, maybe?"

"A radio?" said Ben, and laughed at such foolishness. "No, I should say not. What would he want with a radio?"

A heavy silence was broken by the storekeeper. "That's what I've been telling Ben," he said, addressing the new-comers. "The people have got to make their living from now on by making things with their hands, the way they used to do in the old days. You know, Juliano, how much they used to make—shoes, furniture—the women used to weave and make all kinds of woollen cloth. Well, the Americans will buy that stuff now. They like it. They pay good prices for it, too. Look what Ben's boy has done with his willow chairs."

They all nodded without speaking, and the storekeeper went on full of enthusiasm. And while they talked, two of the visitors got up and walked about the place. For a long time Ben kept his eye on them, but he liked to talk, and before long he was boasting again about his son. They were interrupted at last by the shrill excited voice of Ben's wife from the back of the house, and Ben got up and ran inside.

"You get out of here," the woman was screaming, "I don't want you in my house, go on, get out——" And then Ben's gruff voice: "What do you want in

here? What are you sneaking around my house for?
Get out. Get out, both of you!"

Then Juliano and the other man got up and went
inside, leaving the storekeeper alone in the dooryard.

Juliano pointed accusingly at a gleaming little box
on a table, unmistakably a radio. "What's that?" he
said.

Ben turned about and approached menacingly.
"You get out of here, Juliano Trujillo. You mind
your own business. This is my house. I didn't ask
you to come in. Now you get out——" he swung
around and faced the others. "All of you—get out!"

They went out and met again in front of the house.
And Ben stood in his doorway with doubled fists,
angry.

"Well, *adios*, Ben. That's all we wanted to know."

On the way back down the valley road, the four
men discussed what they had seen, and thought what
to do about it. They'd have to write a letter to the
young women, they agreed. But who could write it?
They'd have to write it in English, wouldn't they?
Who could write in English? None of the four. They'd
have to find some younger man who had been to
school—maybe Cruz could do it, or one of his boys.

They went straight to Cruz's house and found him,
and Cruz thought his oldest boy might be able to do
it. So they found a pencil and a piece of paper and
sat him down at a table.

"What shall I write? I can't write English very good."

"Dear *senoritas*," they dictated, and the boy wrote.

"We telling you about that Ben Ortiz, she taik the mony wan he don need it. Ben, she es mayordomo and get lotsy mony from the pipl, an hes boy, she sell the chars in the town to the Americanos. We want you shud no thes so you don tink we all chete like heem. And we want you stop to geev it to heem, bicos she has got a radio wit you mony."

As none of the four could sign his name, the boy wrote all their names at the foot of the letter, and put it in an envelope.

Ah, that was good! That would put a crease in Ben Ortiz.

The four men went home well pleased. And the next time the young women came to the valley, they spent much time up at Ben's house. When they had gone, Ben came charging down the road full of a tearing rage, stopping at each of the four men's houses, blaspheming and cursing their souls to every shade of purgatory and hell.

If it gave him any comfort, it gave them more. He was especially generous with his cursing of Juliano, whom he considered to blame for the whole affair, and before he left the Trujillo house he had declared everlasting war on the whole breed and consigned

their souls to eternal damnation. The people smiled.
Not one person felt sorry for Ben Ortiz.

Let him live on the proceeds of the willow chairs,
then, if his son was so smart, with his half-witted
brats. Of course some pretended to be sorry—some
who feared to antagonize Ben, as *mayordomo*. And Ben
went home with his hurt somewhat soothed. As he
passed the Trujillo house, walking home, he stopped
and shook his fist at it from the valley road.

CHAPTER V

To feel that a power, however distant, was interested in them again made some of the people lazy and some more industrious. The land was demanding its measure of their lives and out of long habit most of the people went back to work in the fields with new energy. It was harder work than ever because so many horses had died, and so much of the labour had to be done by hand. Some of the families were under-manned, for the boys were enlisting in the conservation camps operated by the government, and their wages were being sent home. Juliano's youngest son—the married one who lived at home—went off to a camp and they got twenty-five dollars every month from him which was more than they could get from the young women at the Welfare Office, and they were content.

It was a new and rather mysterious thing, all these governmental agencies coming into a man's life—especially if you were an old man who had lived always by the labour of your own hands. The young ones took it lightly, as if it were only their due, and cried for more, but the old men like Juliano and Cruz—and poor Beatriz, too, before he died—looked upon it with misgiving. Rumours were now about that the surplus men were to be given work on something called a work project. The valley road, that ancient and rutted thoroughfare, was to be rebuilt, widened and smoothed. It seemed unnecessary. Or they might get a thing called a vocational school, in which the people would be taught again the forgotten arts of the old days. Or they might even dam the stream in the canyon and pipe the water down to the fields. This made sense, for half the water was lost in its meandering down the old ditch whose sandy banks let most of the water escape before it got down to the valley. But they had said before that there wasn't enough water in the stream to bother with.

Anyway, life looked somewhat brighter now, and men held their eyes skyward as they used to do in better days. It was incredible to Juliano that their lives should cease to depend upon the sky. Nothing could ever turn him from his ultimate dependence upon that. His old ears heard tales and alarms, but his eyes sought the meanings of clouds and winds, and watched the horizon as they had done for sixty years and more. He was present at the first irrigating of the cornfield, and his heart was light and his bones felt young again.

Oh, he shouted his orders to the young ones as he used to do when he was young, sloshing barefooted in the mud with a hoe in his hands. All was the same, except now he managed his hoe skilfully with only one hand, and his hair was grey.

They talked as they worked, sliding the water lower and lower in the field, filling one furrow, then the next, a method far more ancient than any man who was working there.

Cruz was beside Juliano, and he was a happy man again. The scene was like so many others out of their past that Juliano was reminded of another time, and he said: "Do you remember, Cruz, the day we were here in this same field and our father died?"

"Yes, I do. It's just like it was then, no? Except the field is smaller—that flood took off the lower end of it."

Juliano straightened his aching back and looked along the field. "It's good we never divided the land among ourselves. The old man was right about that." He dropped his hoe and raised his hand to his mouth. "Hi, you boys—you're losing water down there, can't you see? It's running off into the river!"

"Ah," he said in disgust to Cruz, "these kids don't know anything about irrigating. You'd think they never did it before."

"They haven't done it very much." Cruz was sad again. "Maybe they won't need to know——"

"Oh, yes, they will—and we've got to teach them, Cruz, before we die."

Cruz didn't answer. He felt like a boy himself, beside this old rock of a man, and his strange, stony faith in the land and the sun. Why should this be so? Cruz was only ten years younger. He shook his head, wondering. But it was a truth that he didn't feel as Juliano did about the land—it had failed him too often. Juliano would never agree that the land had failed—it was they who had failed the land, if not directly, then through God who made it.

No, Cruz had seen children sicken and wane through too much dependence on the earth. He didn't trust it any more. Sometimes he hated it, as now he drove his hoe savagely into the mud and muttered a curse upon it which Juliano didn't hear.

Juliano tired quickly. Presently he left the field and sat on the edge of it watching the work of the younger men, and he watched jealously, like a mother guarding her brood. The fragrance of wet earth was sweet in his nostrils, and the sight and sound of water running were joy and music to him. Nothing mattered now. All the pain and anguish of past years fell away. He remembered only the recurring pictures of growing corn and grain, and the sight of the little valley from its rim, the neat pattern of rectangular fields lulled in the bony arms of foothills.

Life in death, that was. Growth and fertility enclosed in the thorny clutch of rock and sand.

Juliano, feeling drowsy in the hot sun, went up to the house and took a nap on his bed.

CHAPTER VI

THE summer, starting with a good moist spring, soon dried and became a hot, noisy affair of grasshoppers and treetoads. On a Saturday, they had the first *baile* the valley had seen in two years, and everybody went to it because it was a sign of better times and they all felt like celebrating.

Juliano was surprised to see so many new faces, so many young boys and girls who had grown up since he went to the last *baile*, and it seemed like a strange community to him all of a sudden. And the place, as he sat dreamily looking on, was peopled again by those whom he had known—Rosa with her sparkling, laughing eyes, Nina, demurely gay, and yes, Ben Ortiz playing the fiddle and leaping down to grab some girl and whirl her around the room a few times. It was easy to fit old faces to new forms, and he sat there thinking.

But it wasn't very like the old dances really. In the first place, he missed the music they used to play; it all sounded unfamiliar now, tunes he had never heard before and the dancing itself was all different, weird clutches and gyrations, embracings and huggings that

shamed a man to look upon. He felt as if he had
stumbled upon an orgy of some kind and was im-
pelled to turn his eyes away.

He did, and studied instead the faces of those older
people who occupied the chairs along the wall, and
the benches where he remembered his grandparents
used to sit, looking on severely. And he had to smile.
It was the same, after all. He and his friends had
simply moved up to the benches. Look at Nina, now.
Wrapped in a black shawl over a black dress, she sat
there watching and not seeing anything. In his sons,
Juliano could see the ghost of Beatriz. No, it was all
the same—only the faces changed.

But how many whom he had known were gone
now! He felt a surge of goodwill towards those who
were left, even for Ben Ortiz, and he got up from his
place and walked over to the bench where Ben was
sitting with his silent, dumpy little wife. A vacant
place beside them seemed to invite Juliano to come
and sit there for comfort in old age.

Ben's wife, after one cold glance, ignored Juliano
altogether, but Juliano's mood was so mellow that he
didn't mind her slight. He leaned across her hemi-
spheric bosom to speak to Ben.

"How do you like this, Ben? Remember when you
played the violin? Why don't you play it now?"

Ben gave him a cold look, too, suspicious, defiant.

"I had to sell my violin," he said.

"That's too bad."

After a long silence between them, Ben leaned across his wife and growled: "Don't try to make friends with me Juliano. It's too late for that. I haven't forgotten what you did to me about the relief money. I won't forget it, either. I'm going to get even with you for that."

And Juliano, suddenly struck by the foolishness of two old men quarrelling like a couple of boys, decided not to reply. He got up and left his place beside Ben's wife and went outside.

Well, he thought, walking home with Nina, guiding her uncertain footsteps in the moonlight, if Ben wants to get even with me he'd better hurry. We'll both be dead pretty soon. I'm an old man—an old, old man. And aloud to Nina he said: "I guess we're too old for *bailes*, Nina."

And Nina, who had before her memory only a blur of moving figures, agreed. "But it's good for the young ones. There hasn't been enough for them to do lately. They get into mischief and do crazy things. They'll have some fights to-night. You'll see."

They had some fights, and some carving with knives. But it was nothing in this strange new world. The doctor came out and fixed the wounds and the boys forgot it all and were friends again when they were sober.

And Juliano had to think how different things might have been if his youth were now instead of fifty years ago. With law and doctors in the land, every man was a king. Why, from a little fight like that at the *baile* came a string of consequences that would have made a man laugh to think about in the old days. A detective came to Vallecito and arrested three boys and took them to the jail in the town. Whoever heard of such a thing? What was the world coming to?

Well, an old man could only sit and watch and wonder and shake his head. It was cool in the *placita*, and Juliano and Nina had much to talk about. Through the summer they sat together every afternoon in the shade of the cottonwoods and found a great companionship between them, going over and over the past, talking and laughing, rattling, aged laughter.

The rains were late. Juliano moved his seat closer to the ditch, so he could watch the water in it, as if it were a prisoner which might escape but for his watching. And he saw it dwindle or quicken as it rained or failed to rain in the mountains above; and his mood varied in accordance with the volume of water there.

In old age, significance dropped from most things. Life for Juliano was reduced to a skeleton of things that mattered. And for Nina too. They often talked about it, but never agreed altogether upon those things which did matter. For Juliano, the water in the ditch was the most important remaining thing in life, and for Nina it was one of the least important. Her grandchildren, it seemed to Juliano, were most important to Nina. He told her that their welfare and their future depended on the water in the ditch, but she only laughed at him.

It was a shock, therefore, to Juliano, when, on an afternoon in August, the boys who had been irrigating the alfalfa came to him in the *placita* and told him a strange story. In the morning, they said, when they started to work there had been plenty of water in the ditch, but as they turned it into the field they noticed that it began to fail.

"Is it our day for the water?" Juliano had said.

They were sure it was.

"We thought something was wrong later when the water stopped altogether, so we went up to see the *mayordomo*—Ben Ortiz—and he was irrigating his beans."

"Did you tell him it was our water to-day?"

"Yes."

"What did he say?"

"He said he didn't care whose water it was, his beans were dry and he was irrigating them."

Juliano heard the words without a change of his remote, thoughtful expression. He settled back in his chair for a time, and then got up and started pacing up and down beside the ditch.

Wrapped in the opaque, upspringing cloud of thoughts which this news induced, Juliano paced up and down beside the ditch, and memories of Ben Ortiz rose like vapours from the ground around him. For a while it was too much for his old brain, this thing that Ben had done.

Stealing water?

But one theft of water was enough to ruin a farm now, when a man got the ditch only once in ten days!

Stealing water! Why, men had been killed for that in Vallecito!

Killed! For the love of God, water was life! Nothing else in the whole waste of rock and sand was as important as that. Oh, the sweet earth! The thirsting earth! What could you say to Ben Ortiz, if you had a tongue to say it with? What could you do to him, if you had arms and the wit to make them go?

You and I, land! You and I against Ben Ortiz. Hasn't it always been like that? I've been your friend, land—I've been faithful to you. I've bowed my head to you, I've served you well, I've sung your praise——

Juliano noticed suddenly that the boys were still standing there, waiting to be told what to do. He took a stand beside the ditch and pointed to the water in it.

267

"Go back," he shouted. "There's water now. Work. Work all night if you have to—the fields must have water!"

He waved them away with a sweep of his arm. "Go back. Work. Work! Give water to the land!"

The boys, sensing something new and compelling in the old man's mood, slipped out of his sight and ran back to the fields.

And Juliano resumed his solitary pacing beside the ditch.

Oh, God! Be my witness in this that I am about to do! I am an old man. I have not long to live. I have borne all things meekly, even the hurts of my enemy. He took my wife and he took my arm, and I forgave him. But I won't let him take water from the land! My good land, my father's and my father's father's land. He can't rob me of that. He can't starve my land, O God!

Oh, how he came in the darkness of my going and stole my Rosa, and poisoned her life and turned her over to the devil. Yes, you did that, Ben Ortiz! You did that, you sneaking, cowardly coyote! You were the one who took my arm away—you turned my Rosa away from me—you made a witch of her, you swine!

Oh, God—Juliano covered his eyes with his hand —I remember thinking once that the land was evil. I saw it closing around me and squeezing me to

268

death. I was afraid of the land. Many times I've been afraid of the land, of its lightning and its floods. The land has threatened me, it has starved me and my children—but always it has forgiven me and relented. Only you are evil, Ben Ortiz! You never forgive. You never relent.

I have been faithful to you, land! I shall be faithful now. I'll save you from this evil, this foul fiend who takes the good, sweet water from you. My land! I'll be true to you, to the end.

Juliano had stopped walking and stood now looking down into the flowing ditch where water slid silently, bending the grasses at its edge. He was trembling from head to foot, and his hand, hanging limply at his side, shook like a leaf in the wind.

Nina came out of the house holding a pail, which she set down on the doorsill. "Is that you, Juliano? Get me some water from the well, will you?"

Juliano didn't move, didn't hear. He raised his head and looked down the valley, along his fields. The boys were working down there, but he didn't see them. I'm going now, land. Thank you for the strength you have given me. Thank you for the food you have given me. Be good to them. Take care of them. They need you. They'll always need you. You will punish them if they fail you, as you have punished me. And I will punish him who has wronged you again and again.

Juliano took a deep breath. Good-bye, my fields, *adios*. Go with God. Whatever happens to me, I have been faithful to you. *Adios*, sky, hills, trees—he looked up—good, strong cottonwoods, *adios*. You have guarded my house well, cottonwoods—go with God.

Juliano walked slowly towards the door of his house. He stepped over the pail Nina had left there, and went in. Without seeing anything else in the room he fixed his eyes on his old rifle hanging on the wall over his bed and walked straight to it from the door, took it down, examined it minutely and walked out again.

Holding his gun swinging at arm's-length, Juliano marched out of the *placita*, down the lane and up the valley road. The evening was cool—he felt its soft caress on his forehead. The land was never so fair. He saw with satisfaction the high standing corn, the beans all heavy with yield, the second thick growth of alfalfa ready to cut. The world was in order again. The land had forgiven them. He was going to protect the land from one who would rob it.

But these things were only the undertone of his thoughts, one with the winding, uneven road, one with the people he passed, who looked back over their shoulders at the strange sight of an old, intent, one-armed man carrying a rifle on a cool summer evening. Some of them laughed at him, at the way he walked along without seeing them or giving any sign that they, too, walked on the valley road.

No, uppermost in his mind was the goal of his duty, the face and figure of Ben Ortiz. He would be sitting in a chair beside his door, and the red rays of sunset would be colouring the adobe wall at his back to the colour of blood. The colour of blood. Everything was the colour of blood now—the hills under the *piñons* and junipers were the colour of blood, the road on which he walked, the dried grasses and weeds beside the road. Wherever the sweet water from the ditch did not go, there was the colour of blood. Only water could wipe out the colour of blood.

The gate leading up to Ben's house from the valley road was shut. Juliano leaned his gun against a fence post while he opened Ben's gate. He closed it again carefully. You never left another man's gate open. And he reached around and picked up his gun, walked deliberately up the knoll to Ben's house.

Long, purple shadows behind the trees, on the hills, a long, gangling shadow marching ahead of him, springing from his feet. The shadow of his gun, foreshortened, looked like a lump of something in his hand.

Juliano strained to see as far as the house, where he could see the red wall shining. But his eyes were old. He couldn't see anything there. He held his gaze fixed upon the red-shining wall, and he drew nearer. At the top of a sharp incline the lane to Ben's house crossed the ditch on a little bridge—and from there Juliano could look into the dooryard.

Yes, Ben was sitting there as Juliano had imagined, but he hadn't heard him yet. Juliano cocked his rifle with his thumb, and advanced, making no effort to conceal himself. While Juliano was still a stone's-throw off, Ben looked up and saw him coming, saw the rifle in his hand. And Ben hurried into his house. When he came out, he, too, had a rifle, and two hands to use it with. He came forward to meet Juliano, slowly, cautiously.

And Juliano, with nothing in his heart except a cold, bitter hate, walked up to Ben and stopped ten feet from him. His eyes thrust their clean, icy gleam into Ben's eyes.

"What do you want, Juliano? What do you mean coming here with a gun? Is it loaded?"

Juliano nodded slowly. "Any man who steals water from me, Ben Ortiz, steals my life. I came to kill you. You're bad. You're not fit to live."

The level intensity of Juliano's voice made Ben shudder. He tried a smile which ended in a twist of abject fear. "I don't know what you're talking about, Juliano. I——"

"Yes, you do. You're a swine, Ben Ortiz. A dirty, sneaking coyote! You're a water-stealer."

Anger came to Ben's rescue. He stepped back,

raising his rifle and cursing. "You're not going to kill——"

Juliano fired from his hip, Ben from his shoulder. The two reports came almost together. Both men straightened, dropped their guns and lunged at each other, swayed for a moment and fell to the ground in a dead embrace that looked grotesquely amiable.

The blood-red sun winked over the top of the western hills, vanished, and the land was bathed in a cooler shade.

THE END

AFTERWORD

Little Valley marks the culmination of Raymond Otis's brief but productive writing career. Like Otis's first two novels—*Fire in the Night* (1934) and *Miguel of the Bright Mountain* (1936), *Little Valley* is set in Santa Fe, New Mexico, and the isolated Hispano villages north of that small capital city. Although he had visited the state several times as a youth, Otis did not settle in Santa Fe before the fall of 1927. Nevertheless, for ten years, until his untimely death on July 13, 1938, his active involvement in numerous civic activities as well as regional Indian and Hispano affairs helped him write realistically and effectively about the plight of rural New Mexicans during the difficult years before and after World War I.

Born in Chicago on May 25, 1900, Raymond Otis was educated at Chicago Latin School and Phillips Andover Academy. He graduated with a bachelor's degree in English from Yale University in 1924, and taught secondary school

Latin before coming to New Mexico in September of 1927. There he met Frances ("Bina") Lindon Smith. They were married on January 21, 1928, in New York City, then returned to Santa Fe to make their home.

Santa Fe of the late 1920s and the 1930s boasted a vigorous arts colony. Among its more illustrious resident writers were Alice Corbin Henderson, Witter Bynner, Haniel Long, Mary Austin, and playwright Lynn Riggs, all of whom befriended Otis in one way or another. In 1933, Long was instrumental in founding Writers' Editions, a cooperative publishing venture involving more than a dozen local poets and authors and utilizing the resources of Walter L. Goodwin, Jr.'s Rydal Press. Although Otis did not himself publish under the Writers' Edition imprint, he was an associate and served as the group's financial secretary.

Raymond Otis also worked for the New Mexico Federal Writers' Project, which was organized under state director Ina Sizer Cassidy in October 1935. Although he wrote some original materials for inclusion in the state guide, much of Otis's FWP service, like that of fellow worker Alice Corbin Henderson, appears to have been as an editor. Nevertheless, several brief descriptions and a twenty-six-page puppet play for children entitled "Tía Sucia" are preserved in the remaining Santa Fe FWP Files.

Santa Feans enjoyed an active little theater during the 1920s and 1930s, and Lynn Riggs, who achieved Broadway and Hollywood success, started his career with the Santa Fe thespians. Otis was a spirited actor and enthusiastic participant in many local productions. In 1937, the Santa Fe Players opened two seasons in their own open-air theater, El Teatro Analco, in the new Santa Fe market and entertainment center called El Parian Analco. Among the productions were Otis's adaptation of Frank Applegate's short story, "San Cristobal's Sheep," and a pre–Santa Fe Fiesta melodrama, "Nellie, the Bandit's Sweetheart, or It Can't Happen in Burro Alley." According to the *Santa Fe New Mexican* of August 27, 1937, the latter "was adapted by Raymond Otis from an old dime novel, and is said to be one of the most hair-raising, breath-quickening, tear-jerking melerdramas yet to be shown here." The article further notes that "the novel from which the masterpiece has been adapted was printed in 1882 . . . [and] it would seem, from perusal of it, that is was written by an Englishman who had never seen Billy [the Kid] nor the Southwest, but who had heard about both. Blood-curdles are never sacrificed to accuracy in either novel or play."

Otis's civic activities were not confined to the stage. His major commitment was to the Santa Fe Volunteer Fire Department, where he served as volunteer, assistant marshal, fire marshal, and president. In 1932, as the organization's "Historian," he wrote a thirty-page printed booklet, "The Santa Fe Volunteer Fire Department: A History of Its Life and Reputation." The group's efforts to quell a large downtown blaze in 1931 structure Otis's first novel, *Fire in the Night* (also published in England by Victor Gollancz, Ltd., as *Fire Brigade*), a sometimes satiric description of small-town Santa Fe's arts colonists as well as its assorted Anglo and Hispano citizens.

Although he served as trustee, member of the Executive Committee, and secretary of the Indian Arts Fund and wrote a thirty-four page illustrated booklet, *Indian Art of the Southwest: An Exposition of Methods and Practices,* distributed by the Southwestern Indian Fair in the 1930s, Otis's deepest concerns were for the poor Hispanic peoples of New Mexico. He worked closely with the League of Spanish-Speaking Workers (La Liga Obrera de Habla Español), and in 1938 the league's state secretary, Luz Salazar, wrote his widow to assure her that: "Together with you, we mourn his death, because with his death the Spanish-American people of New Mexico have lost one of his [sic] sincere and real friends." Otis also maintained close ties with residents of Truchas, an isolated Hispano mountain village north of Santa Fe which is the setting for his second novel, *Miguel of the Bright Mountain*, published in England by Victor Gollancz, Ltd., in 1936.

Vallecito—the "little valley" of this present book, Otis's third and last published novel— is probably based on life in Cundiyó, a tiny community some thirty miles north of Santa Fe. When fieldworkers for the so-called Tewa Basin Study, conducted in 1935 by the Soil Conservation Service, the U.S. Forest Service, and the Office of Indian Affairs, surveyed the village, they found a population of 122, representing 21 families. They described the settlement as follows:

> Cundiyó can be reached over a road . . . [which] for 6½ miles . . . is narrow, steep, stony, ungraded, passable but dangerous . . . . The settlement . . . extends approximately 1 mile up the Rio Frijoles, which at this point forms a series of three pockets or *rincones*

containing holdings of 15, 15, and 30 acres of tillable land. Steep hills surround each of the little valleys, which extend parallel to the southwest border of the grant. The village is beautiful; the houses are plastered with white clay from a local deposit.

The village's two stores had practically no trade, and there were only six cars in the community. Livestock was scarce, and the importance of agriculture, at best uncertain, was indicated by the fact that an annually elected three-member irrigation commission and an irrigation boss were reportedly the only local officials. Also notable in terms of Otis's novel is the statement in the Tewa Basin Study that: "Prior to 1930 all the men left to work in the metal mines of Colorado and Utah, the section-gangs on the Atchison, Topeka, and Santa Fe, and the Denver and Rio Grande Railroads, and as sheep-herders in Colorado and Wyoming . . . the average length of time gone [being] 6 months per year."

Reportedly an admirer of both John Dos Passos and D. H. Lawrence, in *Little Valley* Otis clearly merged the former's realism with the latter's more elemental themes of human passion. Indeed, the vicious consequences of adultery and witchcraft accusations against Rosa almost outweigh the sordid brutalities of the

Colorado mining towns to which she and her war veteran son José eventually "escape." When Rosa returns to her sober, hardworking farmer husband Juliano Trujillo some sixteen years later, his final confrontation with her old lover, dashing fiddler-farmer Ben Ortiz, is made inevitable not only by years of resentment and frustration, but by water, the single inescapable reality of subsistence in a semiarid land.

Like the Lopez family and their Hormiga (Truchas) neighbors, the Trujillos and their fellow Vallecito (Cundiyó) residents were not commercially feasible subjects for fiction in the United States of the 1930s, and both Otis's "village novels" were only published in England. According to Santa Fe (and later Taos) poet, publisher, and "gadfly" Spud Johnson, this unfortunate circumstance led to Otis being known locally as "Our English Novelist." Johnson published a column entitled "The Perambulator" in editor E. Dana Johnson's short-lived *Santa Fe Plaza* weekly. In his inaugural column of August 1, 1937, Johnson introduced his fictional companion "Jasper" and described a trip to Taos, then "even more a colony of writers than of painters," where he saw page proofs of Marina Wister's volume of poems, *Fantasy and Fugue,* Mabel Dodge Luhan's *Edge of Taos*

Desert, and Frank Waters's *Midas of the Rockies.*

However, Taos isn't the only place where proofs on books to be published in the autumn are being anxiously scanned by their authors these hot days. Our own Raymond Otis has a new volume about ready for publication. Here again Jasper was the "discoverer"—he's such a nasty little meddler. We we were up in Ray's new pie-shaped studio which he's just finished and Jasper found on the desk a small paper-bound volume called "Little Valley." He came running up to me with it and screamed:

"Papa, what's a cresset?"

"Shush," I said, "Need you ask before all these people!"

"Yes," he pouted, "Because I've heard of Rotary Presses, but I never heard of a Cresset Press. Tell me what it is."

Sure enough, the book is published by the Cresset Press, London, and the little paper-bound copy was the elegant English version of our messy American "page proofs."

Like *Miguel of the Bright Mountain, Little Valley* was poorly distributed and received almost no notice in the United States. Original editions of both books are now almost impossible to obtain, in all probability because the very limited runs were stored in warehouses bombed during World War II. In effect, then, this reprint makes available for the first time both an important social document and a well-crafted novel by a man whose untimely death in 1938 robbed New Mexico of an active, concerned citizen and deprived the literary world of a skilled and rapidly maturing author.

Marta Weigle
University of New Mexico

Bibliographic Note: A more detailed, annotated account of Otis's life and writings and a fuller description of the Santa Fe writers' colony are in this author's introduction to the Zia reprint of *Miguel of the Bright Mountain* (University of New Mexico Press, 1977). For more on Cundiyó during the 1930s, see the 1935 Tewa Basin Study, reprinted in Marta Weigle, ed., *Hispanic Villages of Northern New Mexico* (Santa Fe: Lightning Tree, 1975); and Ernest E. Maes, "The World and the People of Cundiyó," *Land Policy Review,* March 1941, pp. 8–14. A good historical introduction to witchcraft in the region is Marc Simmons, *Witchcraft in the Southwest: Spanish and Indian*

Supernaturalism on the Rio Grande (Flagstaff, Ariz: Northland Press, 1974; reprint University of Lincoln: Nebraska Press, 1980.)